Runaway
Voyage

Betty Cavanna

Runaway Voyage

William Morrow and Company
New York   1978

Library of Congress Cataloging in Publication Data
Cavanna, Betty (date) Runaway voyage.
    Summary: A fictional account of the mid-19th-century voyage, led by Asa Mercer, of several hundred young women going from the east coast to help populate Seattle. 1. Mercer, Asa Shinn, 1839–1917—Juvenile fiction. [1. Mercer, Asa Shinn, 1839–1917—Fiction. 2. Voyages to the Pacific coast—Fiction] I. Title.
          PZ7.C286Rw   [Fic]   78-17926
ISBN 0-688-22152-1   ISBN 0-688-32152-6 lib. bdg.

Printed in the United States of America.
First Edition
1   2   3   4   5   6   7   8   9   10

79-027

Runaway Voyage

Chapter 1

Very carefully, following Mrs. Endicott's instructions, Eliza dusted the seashell collection kept behind glass doors in the curio cabinet. Today promised to be special, and she wanted nothing to go wrong as a result of her clumsiness.

The shells had been brought back from South America by Mr. Endicott, whom his widow referred to so frequently as "deceased, God rest his soul" that Eliza wondered if he had ever been given a first name. As captain of a small ship engaged in the rubber trade with Brazil, he had gathered many souvenirs that now mingled strangely with the proper mahogany and walnut furniture of the parlor.

Eliza picked up a cone-shaped shell and turned it over in her palm, enjoying the smooth texture and admiring the brown and yellow markings, which reminded her of one of Miss Amelia's silk dresses. She rather hoped the daughter of the house would choose this dress to wear to dinner tonight.

"Eliza! Get on with what you're about, girl. Don't stand there daydreaming when there's work to do."

"Yes, madam."

Although her mistress's voice had caught her by surprise, Eliza answered politely. Work to do, plenty of work, especially when company was coming. Early this morning there had been wood fires to be laid, table silver to be polished, a market errand to run for the cook, besides a myriad of special chores that always accompanied the rare occasion of a guest for dinner. Tonight there would be a gentleman present. A possible suitor for Miss Amelia? wondered Eliza. The prospect of any change in the daily routine was a welcome one, even if it meant extra work.

Amelia Endicott was only two years older than Eliza, yet between seventeen and fifteen there yawned an unbridgeable gap. Miss Endicott, with her curls and crinolines, her ladylike airs, seemed blessed by good fortune to Eliza. Amelia's schooling was finished, and she was of marriageable age. Furthermore, she could move anywhere in Salem society with assurance, in spite of her mother's complaints that the Endicotts were now forced to live in straitened circumstances.

"We now must make do with a cook and a charmaid," Eliza had heard her mistress explain with a sigh. "My husband, deceased, God rest his soul, would be appalled by our paucity of servants."

At least Cook gets paid for the time she puts in, Eliza thought with excusable bitterness, as she finished dusting the exotic shells and closed the cabinet door. As she moved about the room dusting the Chippendale chairs and the impressive Heppelwhite secretary-desk with its gleaming brasses, she wondered what her life would have been like if her father had not died in a factory explosion before the outbreak of the Civil War. Had he lived to fight for the North and march home with the surviving Union soldiers her mother would not have been forced to go to the poorhouse and abandon her daughter to the mercies of the Seaman's Orphan and Children's Friend Society, which operated a home —always referred to as the asylum—on Carpenter Street.

Eliza could summon up only a vague image of her mother. She remembered her as frail and frequently tearful, an impoverished and broken widow who had died in her twenties of consumption, according to the matron at the orphanage.

Because Eliza herself was frail looking, her arms thin, her body childlike, her voice whispering, she had been kept at the asylum well into her twelfth year. And when she was delivered as a bond servant to the steps that led up to the handsome brick house on Chestnut Street, her employer's first words had been, "My, isn't she slight?"

Employer? Eliza smiled ruefully at her hopefulness on that first meeting. Anything—anything—she had believed, would be better than the asylum. Although she looked young for her age, she was achingly aware of the bustling seaport outside the orphanage walls. She was eager to join the throngs in the streets, to begin really living, and the Endicott house seemed to furnish a step toward escape. Later she learned that Mrs. Endicott considered it an act of charity to take her in at all —to provide her with board in the form of leftovers, a room in an unheated attic—although she obviously expected that Eliza would toil from dawn until after dark.

As a twelve-year-old, she had found the household chores not only tedious but physically exhausting. Now, however, she was sturdier and her arms had grown strong. She could lug the firewood up two flights of stairs to Miss Amelia's bedroom without feeling that her arms were ripping loose at the shoulders. She could weather Cook's constant criticism without flinching and could repeat the two required words, "Yes, madam," in her sleep. Yet to this day she had never seen a penny of pay and the prospect ahead was dismal. Somewhere in the depths of her flat little stomach she could feel faint stirrings of rebellion.

"Eliza!"

"Coming, Miss Amelia."

Quick as a wren, Eliza raced up the polished oak treads of Mr. McIntire's handsome staircase. (Samuel McIntire was the famous designer of the house, and no one who lived there was allowed to forget it.) Amelia's bedroom was in more than its usual disorder, because dusk was falling and the dinner guest could be expected shortly. Crushing her stays to her waist with both hands, Amelia said curtly, "Give these a pull, if you please!" and sucked in her breath as Eliza tugged.

"Tighter!"

"I'm afraid I'll break the strings."

Amelia stopped holding her breath. "Tie them then."

Eliza did as she was told, aware that nothing in the world could make a sixteen-inch waist out of one that measured seventeen and a half.

"That'll do." Amelia tucked in the lacings and adjusted the waist of her lace-edged drawers before she stepped into the cage for her crinoline. "Thanks," she said perfunctorily. "That'll be all. I'm sure you're needed downstairs."

I'm needed everywhere, Eliza decided, as she hurried off. The June night was unseasonably cool, so she must light the fire and draw the curtains. In the kitchen Cook would want her to stir the soup. In the dining room she should check the table setting and twist the champagne bottle in its bucket of ice. A grand gentleman must certainly be expected, if he was worthy of the deceased Mr. Endicott's best French champagne!

The *clip-clop* of a horse's hooves signaled the arrival of a hack, and Eliza opened the big front door as soon as the bell jingled. The young man who stood there was slender and bearded, with reddish hair receding at the temples and deep-set dark eyes. He wore sober clothes that looked in need of a press, but he had an engaging manner. "Mrs. Endicott's residence?" he asked in a deep, resonant voice.

"Yes, sir."

"My name is Asa Mercer. I'm a friend of Mrs. Endicott's nephew."

Eliza stood aside. "Please come in."

She took Mr. Mercer's hat and hung it on the brass clothes tree in the hall, then led him into Mrs. Endicott's presence before returning dutifully to the basement kitchen. Later she would be expected to serve the food Cook sent up on the dumbwaiter. When a guest was present, Mrs. Endicott insisted on strict formality, and Eliza had been taught to offer dishes from the left, clear from the right, and never allow a diner to be without a plate in front of him.

The platters as well as the service plates were beautiful but very heavy—celadon decorated with butterflies, brought over on a clipper ship from the Orient by an Endicott engaged in the China trade. It was Eliza's duty to wash them in the soapstone sink, and a chip or a scrape incurred Mrs. Endicott's fury.

"Careless chit!" Eliza had heard her mistress mutter after she had delivered a thorough scolding. "If that girl doesn't start shaping up, I'll send her packing."

Packing what? Eliza had wondered. Aside from the uniform she was wearing tonight, the clothes in her room were the same in which she had arrived from the asylum, although they were threadbare and outgrown. Yet the thought of being returned to the orphanage was even worse than the prospect of continuing in this uncongenial household, and she was determined that tonight she would give no cause for complaint. When Cook sent her upstairs to light the candles and announce that dinner was served, she checked her appearance in the dining-room looking glass to make sure that her braids, usually worn as childish pigtails, were wrapped neatly around her head and that her white apron was not askew. Then she took a long breath and crossed the hall to the parlor door.

"Dinner is ready, madam."

Immediately Eliza realized that nervousness had tricked her into error. How many times had Mrs. Endicott reminded her to say "served" rather than "ready?" This evening, however, she let the slip pass and after a few moments of routine delay arose and led the way to the table.

From her prescribed position at the side of the room near the dumbwaiter Eliza watched Mr. Mercer pull out the ladies' chairs and noted that Miss Amelia was indeed wearing the brown-and-yellow watered silk so reminiscent of the seashell. She looked pretty and plump, but her eyes held no special sparkle. Mr. Mercer apparently didn't measure up to her expectations.

"Since I understand you are a parson, sir, would you care to ask the blessing?" suggested Mrs. Endicott, then lowered her eyes to stare down at her empty service plate while the guest delivered a long and predictable grace.

After he finished, Mr. Mercer said quickly, "I hope your nephew didn't misinform you, ma'am. While I am indeed a man of the cloth I am not currently practicing my calling. You might say I wear several hats, because I serve in the Washington territorial legislature and have also been instrumental in founding a university in Seattle."

"Seattle?" mused Amelia, as Eliza served the soup. "Isn't that in Canada?"

"Close to it, on Puget Sound," replied Mr. Mercer with a smile. "In other words, in the far West."

Mrs. Endicott's expression turned thoughtful. "My nephew mentioned that you came from Washington Territory. You wouldn't—you couldn't!—be the same young man who spoke at the Mechanics' Hall in Lowell last year, seeking to carry off young girls from New England to—" She stopped abruptly, looking distraught.

Mr. Mercer laughed. "The very same!" he said proudly. "But your shocked expression does me a disservice, Mrs. Endicott. The eleven young ladies who embarked under my chaperonage to Seattle were of impeccable character, and I can report that they are now happily settled as schoolteachers, milliners, and—"

"Wives?" interrupted Amelia with sudden interest.

"Indeed, yes!" replied Mr. Mercer with an ingratiating smile.

"Mmph," muttered Mrs. Endicott.

The gentleman turned back to his hostess. "You see, ma'am, the ratio of men to women in the territory is a hundred to one. It is only natural that a group of virgins and war widows from the ages of fifteen to twenty-five would be quickly married."

Amelia looked even more interested. At the first opportunity she asked, "What is Seattle like, Mr. Mercer? Is it a thriving city?"

"Thriving, yes, but scarcely a city. At this stage it is still a frontier town, although soon we hope to have paved streets, some decent stores, even a grammar school." He finished his soup, then said with a chuckle, "Up to now there have been very few children about, except for those of the Indians and half-breeds."

Mrs. Endicott's sniff was clearly audible. "Just as I thought," she said. "Yet you claim that self-respecting New England girls left home to emigrate to such a God-forsaken place?"

Eliza flinched at the insult, almost as if it had been directed at her, but Mr. Mercer seemed unperturbed. He helped himself to fish from the platter she held, then replied, "One must not be too harsh, ma'am. Seattle is young, but it is vigorous and full of opportunity. Such defects as now exist will be corrected as more ladies of quality move west." He glanced at Amelia with a sparkle in his eye.

"Well!" said Mrs. Endicott rather sharply. "We shall see what we shall see."

"You will admit, Mama," said Amelia from across the table, "that the war has taken most of our eligible young men. Why, Grace Vickery was saying just the other day that to find husbands she and her three sisters might well search the graveyards."

"Amelia!" Although Eliza thought the remark showed unusual spirit, Mrs. Endicott's cry was horrified. She apparently thought the conversation was getting out of hand and tried to change the subject.

Mr. Mercer, however, had other ideas. Undaunted, he launched on a description of his current project. "It's very clear," he said, "that times are hard here in the East, while in the West there is great prosperity.

I've been attempting this year to arrange a far greater migration of young women interested in financial improvement. President Lincoln had promised me a ship, but alas on the very day I reached New York he was assassinated."

"God rest his soul," said Mrs. Endicott. Then she added, not without satisfaction, "So you must give up the plan?"

"No, indeed! General Grant, who has soldiered in the West and knows how urgently good women are needed out there, has recently promised me a troopship."

"Well!" said Mrs. Endicott again.

"Will young ladies find a troopship sufficiently comfortable?" asked Amelia, as Eliza removed the fish plates.

"It will be converted to suit their needs," promised Mr. Mercer confidently, then leaned forward as though he were about to divulge a fascinating secret. "I must tell you ladies that I am having great good fortune during my trip through Massachusetts. Quantities of young women are responding eagerly to my invitation to sign up, because I can guarantee employment as soon as my volunteers arrive in Seattle. The minimum salary," he said with emphasis, "will be four dollars a week—in *gold*. You'll agree that's more than a living wage!"

"In *gold*?" cried Amelia, clasping her hands. "My, doesn't that sound exciting, Mama?"

"Exciting, perhaps, but dubious."

"How so, ma'am? Already I have nearly four hundred girls ready and anxious to board ship with me!"

"Anyone from Salem?" questioned Amelia eagerly, as she followed her mother's lead and picked up her knife and fork to start on the main course.

"Several," Mr. Mercer replied. "Among them Miss Thankful Turner, whom you undoubtedly know."

Mrs. Endicott made a sound that was remarkably close to a snort. "Her parents will be thankful to be rid of that one," she said briskly. "The girl's been nothing but trouble since the day she was born."

"Mama, aren't you being a trifle cruel?" Amelia demurred.

"If honesty is cruelty, so be it."

"Time will tell," said Mr. Mercer soothingly. "In any event, it appears that Miss Turner has an adventurous spirit." He turned to Amelia. "As I believe you have also, if I may pay you the compliment."

"Amelia gets desperately seasick," her mother said quickly. "And as for being adventuresome, I must hasten to disagree. My daughter has never been farther away from Salem than Boston, and even on that short train journey she turned queasy. No, I think we must leave adventure to more robust young ladies, Mr. Mercer." She nodded to Eliza, who was listening to every word, and indicated that it was time to serve the dessert.

The floating island, as Cook called the pudding, looked creamy and delicious to Eliza, although she feared there would be none left over to take back to the kitchen. Mr. Mercer took an ample portion, then smiled up at her. "Don't tell me you made this!"

Eliza shook her head, although she could have told him that she had often been entrusted with the task of stirring the custard. At the same time Mrs. Endicott said, "Our cook will be pleased to hear that you enjoy *oeufs à la neige*." She used the phrase self-consciously, as though she didn't quite trust her accent.

Amelia, who had refused the pudding, accepted a second glass of champagne. Her cheeks were becomingly flushed as she took several sips of wine, then leaned forward to ask Mr. Mercer, "Will you be sailing from Boston harbor or from New York?"

"From New York," said the young man affably. "We have announced no sailing date as yet, but if all goes well the ship should be ready by the middle of August, so we would get under way soon after." He hesitated a moment, then asked boldly, "Is it too much to hope, Miss Amelia, that you might care to come along?"

About to pass the dessert for the second time, Eliza was moving toward Mrs. Endicott. She knew what Amelia was bound to reply—or rather what her mother would indubitably reply for her. The suggestion might sound tempting, but of course acceptance was out of the question—utterly unthinkable. One might as well invite Amelia to join a Gypsy caravan!

Nevertheless, the opportunity Mr. Mercer was offering seemed so provocative, so utterly dazzling to Eliza that she felt suddenly weak, almost faint. The Waterford crystal bowl containing the remnants of the pudding slipped from her hands uncontrollably and shattered into a hundred pieces on the polished oak floor.

Chapter 2

Life became even more difficult for Eliza following the episode of Mr. Mercer's visit. About the breaking of the crystal bowl she was truly contrite, apologizing with the utmost sincerity, although she did not weep as expected. Fortunately, Mrs. Endicott's wrath was lessened by a running argument with her daughter, whose imagination had been fired by Mr. Mercer's eloquence.

Amelia remained intrigued by the thought of new worlds to explore. "What is there for me here?" she asked her mother in Eliza's hearing. "Leftovers from the war! George Bowen has a wooden leg. Walter Proctor lost an eye at Gettysburg."

"Noble scars, earned in battle!" retorted Mrs. Endicott. "You should be proud that young men from Salem served the North so well."

"I am proud, Mama, but I don't want to marry either one of them, and I don't care a whit if they did go to Boston Latin and Harvard."

Eliza could see that the possibility of finding an acceptable husband would have lured Amelia to the ends of the earth, which is precisely where Mrs. Endicott placed Seattle. "Ridiculous!" she scoffed. "Thankful Turner could find a husband right here if she wanted to—she's pretty enough!—but she's always been flighty, ever since she was a child. Flighty and headstrong, both!"

"Oh, Mama! Why have you taken such a dislike to Thankful? When I was little, you always said she acted like a perfect lady."

"She still does," said Mrs. Endicott. "But acting isn't *being*. Thankful has a shrewd eye on the main chance, and she has taken it into her head to believe Mr. Mercer's claim that the Western wilderness offers more opportunity than New England. Well, she's wrong!"

For the next few weeks the sound and the fury of the clash penetrated the farthest reaches of the house, and Amelia's unexpected willfulness distracted her mother from the notion of sending Eliza back to the asylum. Upon occasion she called the housemaid an "ungrateful wretch," but concerning the accident to the Waterford bowl she took no specific action.

Amelia stormed and sulked. She went on an eating spree and consumed an entire box of sweets presented by one of her infrequent admirers. She dared to call her mother old-fashioned and rigid, criticisms Eliza considered just although ill-advised. Amelia even predicted that she'd end up an old-maid piano teacher, a fate that seemed to Eliza far from terrible. Indeed, to be so preoccupied with husband-hunting appeared more than a little silly to an orphan with no prospects whatever.

"That young lady doesn't know how lucky she is," declared Cook one afternoon. "Just suppose *you* could trade places with her, girl!"

To her own surprise, this rather mean-spirited suggestion provoked no envy in Eliza's heart. She didn't want to be anyone but herself.

However, to contemplate a lifetime working as a servant in this or another Salem household was unthinkable. The schooling Eliza had received during her years in the asylum had stimulated her mind and made her eager to learn more. She liked to read; she was good at arithmetic; spelling was easy and fun. With further education she might have become a schoolteacher working with children, helping their minds to expand and grow.

A modest enough ambition, Amelia would have thought, but one that Eliza automatically thought of in the past tense. Her years at school had been too few: Such a prospect was beyond possibility. Now that she was fifteen, work was the only promise the future offered, and housework at that.

One sweltering August night Eliza lay in bed in her room under the roof and sized up her abilities. Under Cook's direction she had learned to prepare simple dishes, she had been taught by Mrs. Endicott to clean house, and she had learned to iron really well. Yes, of all her chores she was best at ironing. If times weren't so hard, she might dare to leave and seek a job in a laundry—a job that paid!

While appealing, the idea wasn't really practical. Most laundresses probably had homes to return to at night, while she would have to rent a room and buy her own food. She might as well dream, like Amelia, of emigrating to the West.

Certainly servants must be needed in Seattle, as they were everywhere else in the country. If only there were some way of getting there! According to the *Salem Gazette*, Mr. Mercer's expedition was due to sail on August 19, just a few days from now. Eliza lay with her hands clasped under her head and dreamed of being spirited to New York, smuggled aboard ship, and arriving before Christmas at a destination as far from New England as it was possible to get on this continent.

Of course, it was only a dream, and dreams were cheap. The sailing date came and went, Mrs. Endicott breathed a sigh of relief, and Amelia left off moping for a lost opportunity. In September came a hurricane that sank a number of ships and led Mrs. Endicott to remark, "There, you see!"

She spoke too soon, because as Eliza learned through another newspaper paragraph Mr. Mercer's plans had gone awry. The New York quartermaster general declared that General Grant had acted without authority in promising the loan of a military transport and refused to allow a Government vessel to transport a cargo of females *anywhere*.

"There, you see!" said Mrs. Endicott to Amelia once more.

Quite naturally, a great many girls who had signed contracts with Mr. Mercer got tired of waiting. Others ran out of money, and those who had been poor to begin with came back to New England to seek employment in the mills of Boston and Lowell, which were opening up again in the autumn of 1865.

Eliza stayed put. She fretted; she was increasingly restless, but she had nowhere to go. Walter Proctor, looking haggard but resigned, came to call on Amelia. Eliza found his black eye patch rather romantic, but Amelia tossed her curls and played the piano rather than sit beside him on the sofa as Eliza thought she should.

October came, with its blowing leaves and brush fires, November with the inevitable Thanksgiving dinner shared by various Endicott relatives, December with snow and cold and Christmas wreaths of balsam fir decorating front doors along Chestnut Street. Eliza continued to perform her daily tasks with apparent composure, while Amelia took to having vapors. She cried a lot. "Because I'm unhappy," she told her mother. Mrs. Endicott, in response, invited a number of young people to musical evenings at which her daughter could perform.

Right after Christmas Amelia began to take singing lessons, and "the little brown church in the grrr-een-wood, the little brown church in the vale" echoed through the house. Her high soprano made Cook nervous. She complained to Eliza, developed migraine headaches, then unexpectedly gave notice. "There's no help for. it," Mrs. Endicott said. "Until I can find a replacement, Eliza, you'll just have to do your best."

Housework, laundry, and now cooking! Eliza's best, as she herself recognized, was not very good. Without Cook's supervision she was unable to manage the big coal stove and bring even the simplest vegetables and meats to the point where they were all ready to serve at the same time. The meals she prepared were barely edible, and the tension in the household increased from day to day.

One afternoon early in the new year Grace Vickery came to visit Amelia, who was confined to the house with a bad cold. As she brought tea into the parlor Eliza heard the guest say that her mother was looking for a laundress who could "live in" and do the family wash. The next morning, making a detour on her way to market, Eliza gathered her courage and approached the big Vickery house on Federal Street to apply for the job.

The servant who answered the door looked dumbfounded when Eliza, her empty market basket slung over her arm and her outgrown orphanage coat unbuttoned, asked if she could speak to the madam. If Mrs. Vickery herself hadn't come into the hall at that moment, Eliza might have been turned away.

The lady hesitated, then came forward. "You want to see me?"

Eliza nodded. As the servant retired she explained in a rush that she wanted to apply for the position of laundress. "I know how to wash, and I iron quite nicely," she said.

"Really? Where did you learn?" asked Mrs. Vickery, eying Eliza's childish figure.

"First at the asylum, then—" Eliza broke off, gulped, and continued, "Where I work now."

"And where is that?"

"At the Endicotts'," Eliza admitted. "But Mrs. Endicott took me straight from the orphanage, and she doesn't pay. I need to work for wages."

"How old are you, child?"

"Going on sixteen," said Eliza.

"You don't look it."

"Maybe not, but I'm strong."

Mrs. Vickery was sympathetic. "And ambitious," she said gently. "But it would be out of the question for me to hire a girl away from a friend's house. Surely you can understand that?"

Such an objection had never occurred to Eliza, but she recognized its validity. She bit her lip unhappily, swept by the realization that virtually every door in Salem would be closed to her for the same reason. Mrs. Endicott knew everybody of means. What a fool she had been to seek this path of escape!

Once back outside she hurried toward Essex Street and the market district while her eyes stung with unshed tears. She filled her basket with potatoes and cabbage, sugar and tea, along with a small halibut which the fishmonger wrapped in a page torn from an old issue of the *Gazette*. Not until she was back in the Endicotts' kitchen and preparing the fish for dinner did she happen to glance at the close-set type and discover, by sheer coincidence, a news item about the Mercer expedition.

Eliza read the short paragraphs eagerly. Mr. Mercer apparently had worked his way out of his difficulties and was reported to have arranged for transportation of his party aboard a steamer called the S. S. *Continental*, scheduled to sail from New York to the West Coast on January 16. Today was the twelfth.

Although the newspaper was sodden and smelly, Eliza tore the item out and crammed it into her apron pocket, then went ahead with cleaning the fish.

"Eliza!"

"Yes, madam?"

"Didn't you hear the front doorbell?"

"No, madam."

"Well, answer it, please," called Mrs. Endicott down the well of the dumbwaiter.

"Yes, madam." Eliza washed her hands and hurried upstairs.

Thankful Turner stood on the doorstep, bundled up against the bitter January wind. Her blond hair was becomingly tousled, her cheeks were pink, and her eyes were shining. "I've come to see Miss Amelia," she told Eliza, "to say good-bye."

So Thankful hasn't given up the trip, thought Eliza, as she showed her into the parlor. In less than a week she'll be standing on shipboard with dozens of other girls who have enough spunk to head west. Amelia was bound to be green with envy, even though she might not admit it to Thankful's face.

Eliza lurked near the parlor door, pausing to dust the highboy in the hall, so that she could overhear the girls' conversation. "I'm taking the train to Boston, then going by boat to New York. Papa's going to see me to Boston. Then in New York one of Mr. Mercer's helpers will meet me. Doesn't that sound thrilling, Amelia? I wish you were coming too."

"Mama would never allow me to be met by a total stranger," said Amelia with a show of sedateness. "Why, you don't even know whether it will be a man or a woman Mr. Mercer will send."

Thankful giggled. "I hope it'll be a man, and a young one at that," she said in an audible whisper. "I'm tired of sitting around Salem with nothing to do but crochet."

"Write to me," Amelia begged. No longer able to conceal her envy, she urged, "Tell me all about Seattle. Then if Mr. Mercer takes another shipload of girls west next year, maybe I'll be able to convince Mama to let me go."

"A year is practically forever," Thankful said with a shrug. "By then, Amelia, you"ll be eighteen—and I expect I'll be married!" She smiled to herself, then added magnanimously, "But I'll write you anyway."

When Eliza let Thankful Turner out the front door she almost wished her a pleasant voyage, then remembered in time that she was not supposed to have been eavesdropping. As soon as her friend had left, Amelia dashed upstairs, holding her crinoline high so she wouldn't trip. A moment later the door of her bedroom slammed behind her.

Poor Amelia! She can't slam the door on the future, Eliza mused as she peeled potatoes. Why does she continue to wail and rage against fate? If I were in her shoes, I'd *do* something!

The kernel of an idea started to form in Eliza's brain. If she could just get to the ship—!

During the past few weeks Eliza had given up dreaming. No good genii would spirit her to New York. She'd have to get there on her own. And once on the dock from which the *Continental* was to sail her problems would only begin. She couldn't expect Mr. Mercer to transport her to Washington Territory free of charge, but perhaps she could persuade him to let her work for her passage. The young ladies aboard would certainly need their dresses and underwear laundered, and almost as certainly this detail might be one a busy gentleman could overlook.

The crux of the matter, of course, was money. How much would it cost to take the train from Salem to Boston and the overnight boat to New York? Thankful would know, but Eliza dared not ask her. Instead, after marketing the next morning, she raced to the railroad station, an impressive granite building with towers that made it look like a castle, and approached the ticket seller to inquire timidly the carfare to Boston.

"Forty-five cents," the bespectacled clerk told her. "Want a train schedule?"

"Please, sir."

Eliza turned away, then went back to the window. "Would you happen to know what the night boat to New York costs? The cheapest passage."

The man scratched behind his ear with the unsharpened end of his pencil. "I couldn't rightly say, but it's not too dear." He glanced at Eliza's shabby clothes and asked, "You plannin' on takin' a trip?"

"I'm inquiring for a friend," Eliza explained in her whispering voice, hoping the fib was excusable. She left the station building and started back toward Chestnut Street, then changed her mind and stopped at a newspaper stand to buy a *Boston Transcript* with a copper from Mrs. Endicott's purse.

Eliza realized that she was stealing. Guilt pursued her all the way back to the house, and she hid the newspaper under her coat as she went in the basement door to the kitchen. Not until she could get to her room after the dinner dishes were finished did she have a chance to turn the pages and search for an advertisement that might give her the information she needed.

Fortunately, her guess was a good one. The sailing time of the night boat was listed, along with fares for cabin-class and deck passengers. When Eliza added the cost of the boat trip to that of the train fare to Boston, the sum amounted to more than three dollars, as much as she spent on a week's marketing for the Endicotts.

A week's marketing! Suddenly Eliza knew where she might get the money. Her heart pounded. Because she had stolen the penny for the newspaper was she starting on the road to perdition? Theft was a sin. Theft was also a crime, punishable by a prison sentence, as the matron at the asylum had repeatedly warned.

Eliza folded the newspaper and hid it under the mattress, then pulled the covers around her neck. Even so, her teeth chattered. How could she contemplate such a low act as running off with the money from Mrs. Endicott's household purse?

Yet she did contemplate it. She persuaded herself she could merely borrow the sum she needed and return the amount by mail when she reached the Washington Territory and found a paying job. What was the sum Mr. Mercer had promised the girls could earn? Four dollars a week—in *gold!* Why, she'd be able to send Mrs. Endicott the money almost as soon as she arrived in Seattle. Then her conscience would be clear.

But suppose she was caught before she even reached the *Continental?* Runaway bond servants were pursued relentlessly by the police, Eliza had been told. And besides being a runaway, she would be a thief!

A grim midwinter moon, almost full, shone accusingly from the sky above Salem, its light slipping through the window to touch the corner of the bed pillow. Eliza clenched her hands and tried to gather courage, but the prospect of deliberate wrongdoing was terrifying. After a sleepless night she crept downstairs and went about her morning tasks as usual, although her mouth was dry with apprehension. How could she consider such a course? A dozen things could go wrong. She could be hauled back to Salem ignominiously and thrust into jail like a common criminal, far worse off than before.

She set up the breakfast trays, poured the tea, made the toast, and took them to the upstairs bedrooms. Mrs. Endicott was alert and impatient. "You're ten minutes late," she said. Amelia, on the other hand, was still asleep. She turned over drowsily when Eliza opened the door and gestured toward the foot of the bed. "Just put it there."

Neither of the Endicotts would dream that the slip of a girl who waited on them so demurely was wondering how she could get her hands on the market money. Eliza felt doubly guilty because they were unaware of her secret thoughts. She went back downstairs with the feeling that time, measured by the tall clock in the front hall, was racing out of control.

Today was the fourteenth of January. Either she must be on the boat to New York tonight or not at all, because who could tell at what hour on the sixteenth the *Continental* would sail? Eliza went into the parlor and stood before the desk where Mrs. Endicott kept her purse, then deliberately grasped the brass handles of the top drawer and tugged.

The drawer was locked! She might have expected it. Mrs. Endicott was a cautious woman and a careful housekeeper without (as she put it repeatedly) "money to throw around." The other desk drawers could be opened, but they contained nothing but ledgers and papers. Eliza's heart fell.

The hall clock struck the half hour. Nine thirty, the time at which Mrs. Endicott usually presented her marketing list. At the sound of footsteps Eliza hurried out to the hall, but it was only Amelia trailing downstairs in a morning coat with lace-edged sleeves.

In spite of her perturbation Eliza noticed that Amelia looked a trifle peaked. She was carrying her breakfast tray and asked if there was hot water on the stove.

"Yes, miss. Would you like me to make more tea?"

"No. I'll get it," said Amelia rather surprisingly. She set the tray on the dumbwaiter in the dining room, then went on down to the kitchen, holding up the skirt of her morning coat with both hands.

"Eliza—"

"Yes, madam." Here was Mrs. Endicott now, marketing list in hand, but the small amount of money she would dole out offered no hope of escape. She went to the desk, unlocked the top drawer, and took out the familiar silk purse. "Five cents for rice, twenty-five cents for a pound of beefsteak, and—"

A piercing scream suddenly split the air. From the basement kitchen Amelia's voice was shrill with alarm. Eliza turned and flew downstairs two steps at a time, Mrs. Endicott not far behind her.

Still screaming, Amelia was standing between the stove and the kitchen table, trying to rip off her morning coat. The entire right sleeve was ablaze.

Eliza did the first thing that entered her head. She seized the pitcher of cold water that stood on the table and dashed it over the frantic girl. There was a sizzle, a sputter, a gasp of outrage from Amelia, but at least the fire was out.

"You didn't have to soak me!" Amelia cried, her teeth chattering. Instead of being grateful, she was furious.

"Let me see your arm," her mother ordered, as the odor of searing flesh penetrated the room.

"Good Lord!" Mrs. Endicott's most extreme expletive started Amelia sobbing. Shock, until now, had made her unaware of pain.

"Eliza, run for the doctor. Tell him it's an emergency. This burn must be seen to at once." She pulled the sleeve away from the scorched skin gently and helped her daughter out of her dripping robe. To Eliza she commanded, "Hurry, girl!"

The doctor lived only around the corner. He was seeing a patient in his office but came to the Endicotts' as quickly as possible. Eliza let him in and showed him upstairs, then returned to the kitchen to clean up.

The purse was the first thing that met her eyes. Mrs. Endicott's purse, plump with the week's house money. Left forgotten on the kitchen table, it was her reprieve from a life sentence of servitude—or so she hoped!

Chapter 3

Counting on the probability that the doctor would need some time to dress Amelia's burns, Eliza crept quietly up to her attic room. She opened a square of plaid cotton on her bed, quickly piling her few possessions in the center—a change of underwear, her striped summer dress, two well-darned pairs of woolen stockings. Then she tied the corners together crosswise, making a convenient bundle-handkerchief out of it. Amelia's moans, the doctor's comforting voice, and Mrs. Endicott's sharper tones, coming from beyond the half-open bedroom door, reassured Eliza as she hurried back downstairs.

The purse still lay on the kitchen table. She picked it up, glanced at its contents, but didn't take time to count the money. There should be enough.

A moment later she left the house, shutting the kitchen door quietly behind her. Big, thick snowflakes were falling through the air, gathering underfoot on the brick pavement and deadening the sounds of horses' hooves and her own racing footsteps. Salem had never seemed so quiet to Eliza—ominously quiet. She ran through the streets with her coat clutched about her and the bundle-handkerchief swinging against her side.

The wind had become sharp, the cold biting, and by the time the turreted train station appeared through the falling snow Eliza's breath was coming in short, painful jerks. Every person she passed seemed a threat, a potential accuser. Thief! whinnied a dray horse; thief! whistled a foghorn on a boat leaving the harbor. Mrs. Endicott's purse, tucked securely into her deep apron pocket, felt like a grocer's leaden weight as it banged against her thigh.

The station house was almost empty at midmorning, businessmen bound for the city long since gone. Few women were lured into making excursions in such treacherous weather, so Eliza felt especially exposed as she bought her ticket. The man behind the grilled window did not recognize her, however, and she dared to ask the time of the next train.

"Twenty minutes, miss," came the muttered reply, and Eliza turned away with breathless thanks. She forsook the warmth of the waiting room and huddled in a corner outside the door, peering along a track all but hidden by snow as though her deep anxiety might hasten the arrival of the train.

The minutes passed so slowly that Eliza's teeth began to chatter, as much from nervousness as from the cold. A man pushing a handcart piled high with boxes marked for Boston glanced her way and said, "You better get inside, girl, before you catch your death," but she didn't stir. It seemed as though an hour passed, as though the train would never come.

At last, however, it rumbled into the station, wheezing and belching black smoke. An old man with a cane was the only other passenger boarding in Salem. He was a stranger to Eliza, for which she gave silent thanks.

Huddled in the nearest empty seat, she brushed at the snow that had settled on her coat and wriggled her freezing toes inside her boots, the soles of which had worn pitifully thin. Now the heavy lump of Mrs. Endicott's purse felt reassuring. She finally gathered enough courage to take it out of her pocket and count the remaining money—three dollars in bills, ten cents in change—although she was afraid someone would be watching suspiciously. Afraid, knowing for the first time how criminals must feel.

Houses whirled by on one side of the track; black water roiled on the other. Factories and warehouses appeared as the city drew closer and the snow gradually turned to freezing rain. Finally the train pulled into a long, dark station, sliding past other trains ranged along a wooden platform. "Last stop!" called the conductor. Then he glanced at Eliza and added for good measure, "Everybody off."

Shrinking into her coat in the hope of not being noticed, Eliza followed the few other passengers down the slippery train steps, trailed along in their wake to a waiting room that seemed huge by Salem standards, and finally gathered courage to approach a uniformed

porter and ask where she might find the boat from
Boston to New York.

"Ain't no boat from Boston," came the offhand reply. "You got to walk over to Kneeland Street and
take the train to Stonington. She leaves from the pier
there about five o'clock."

Eliza's eyes widened in dismay. "How do I get to
Kneeland Street?"

"Walk out that door there, go straight ahead, and
ask anybody in Haymarket Square."

And Stonington. "Where is Stonington?" Eliza was
about to ask, but the man had turned away and she
was left to follow his directions as best she could,
eventually reaching another station and boarding another train that required a whole dollar of her precious
money. Belatedly she remembered that the *Transcript*
advertisement had specified the Stonington Line, but
she had been misled by Thankful Turner into asso-
ciating the name with Boston.

The train rattled along busily, stopping at several
village stations and passing through wintry farmlands.
Eventually Eliza learned from the conductor that
Stonington was a port town on the Connecticut coast,
all the way across Rhode Island from Massachusetts.
Time passed in fits and starts, jerking Eliza awake if
she dozed, reminding her that she was hungry, warning her that she must remain on guard. Not even
when she reached New York would she be out of
danger.

At Providence, a sizable city, a number of travelers climbed on board, surrounding themselves with

valises, portmanteaus, and baskets of food at which Eliza glanced enviously. A man passed up and down the aisle, carrying sandwiches on a tray strapped around his neck, but she dared not spend a nickel until she was sure the two dollars and ten cents remaining in Mrs. Endicott's purse would see her safely aboard the boat to New York. Instead, she shrank into the corner of her seat and gazed out the smoky window with a show of interest she did not feel.

Reaction was setting in. As flat fields of corn stubble sped past, Eliza felt more frightened and alone than ever. Yet she couldn't regret her actions, even the theft of the money. She had written the full amount down with the pencil she carried in her apron pocket: three dollars and fifty-five cents, the price of freedom.

Keep that in mind, she cautioned herself, and she also kept in mind the alternative: endless years stretching ahead in Salem, years with no hope of bettering her position beyond perhaps someday becoming a cook. She shuddered, remembering Cook's arthritis, her migraine headaches, her "miseries," undefinable ailments that caused her to sniffle and complain. Any fate would be preferable, Eliza persuaded herself staunchly, than to grow old and wretched like Cook.

"How long before we get to Stonington?" a lady with a feathered bonnet asked the conductor after another half hour. She was sitting in the seat ahead of Eliza, and her voice had an imperious ring.

"We're running a bit late, ma'am, but there's no

need to worry," the conductor replied soothingly. "The boat always waits for the train."

Relieved, Eliza straightened her back and stretched a little. As the train lurched along its wheels seemed to pick up the rhythm of a familiar spiritual, the refrain of which echoed in Eliza's head. "One more river to cross—"

"Last stop!" called the conductor eventually. "Everyone off!"

Following the lady with the feathered bonnet down the steps and along the wooden platform, Eliza once more felt sick with fear that the money remaining in Mrs. Endicott's purse might prove too little to buy even the cheapest passage to New York. But with relief she found that deck passengers had to pay only two dollars, since the train fare was apparently counted in with the cost of the trip. She handed over the money, glanced ruefully at the single small coin that remained in the purse, and scurried up the gangplank in search of a dim corner where she might pass the night unobserved.

While the boat steamed along the Connecticut coast in the early dark the more affluent hurried to the dining salon and the others opened bags and baskets containing food. The odors assaulted Eliza's nostrils as she crouched with her cold feet drawn under her too-short skirt and the bundle of clothing clasped against her stomach, but she tried to ignore even the thought of hunger. After a while she dozed and toward midnight finally fell asleep.

The stirring of other passengers awakened her shortly after daylight. Stiff and sore, she found her way to the washroom and managed to brush her teeth and comb her hair. Meanwhile, the boat was edging past wharves lining a busy river, finally turning to pull up to a dock of its own.

Huddled among talkative strangers, Eliza ventured close to the rail. "The North River ain't what it used to be," an elderly man said to a companion. "Look at this traffic! I can remember when West Street was more like a country road."

"All ashore!" shouted a blue-clad officer, as the gangplank was lowered, and along with the rest of the deck passengers Eliza crowded forward. An almost feverish excitement captured her as she was swept along. New York! She was in New York!

Piers lined West Street as far as the eye could see. Vessels of every description cluttered the waterfront—coal barges, sailing ships, side-wheelers, steamboats, ferries. The cobbled thoroughfare facing the piers was crowded not only with people but with hundreds of carts and carriages. There were horsecars, broughams, beer wagons, landaus, even a flat-bed vehicle hauling a big dory. Barrels were being unloaded from freighters and stacked on the wharves. Luggage was being carried from private carriages to various boats, trunks were being hoisted to the shoulders of stalwart longshoremen. Flags were flying, dogs were barking, people were hurrying here and there, and into the midst of the melee came Eliza, to stand and read the signs on the shipping sheds: *Cromwell for New Orleans,*

Dispatch Line Philadelphia, Outside Line for Boston, but where could she find the *Continental,* bound for San Francisco and Seattle?

Urgency made Eliza approach half a dozen likely informants, but they shook their heads or passed her along to another source.

"Try Pier 7."

"Perhaps Pier 11."

She wove through the throng determinedly, asking her question again and again. "The *Continental?* Mr. Mercer's expedition."

At last a carter said, "Ah!" and a big grin spread over his pockmarked face. "You one of his virgins, lass?" He pushed back his cap, winked slyly, and pointed south. "Keep going right past the Savannah and Charleston Line and look for Pier 2. She's sailing at last. Today, I hear tell."

Eliza was off at a run before the man had finished speaking. What if she should be too late? The *Continental,* however, was still snug in her berth, although the confusion surrounding the ship was feverish. Girls in crinolines were picking their way up the gangplank, porters were staggering under trunks and bandboxes, an express wagon hauled by straining horses was being edged as close as possible to the side of the ship. Leaning over the rail were excited young women standing on tiptoe, trying to spot their belongings among the welter of luggage. Nobody noticed a childish figure in a threadbare coat who carried a bundle clasped to her breast.

Eliza took a deep breath and scurried up the gangplank in the midst of a bevy of girls. Nobody stopped her. Nobody paid any attention to her at all. "Where can I find Mr. Mercer?" she asked a deckhand, but the fellow couldn't say. "You might try the captain's office, but it's more than likely Mr. Mercer's keeping out of sight today."

"Why is that?"

The deckhand didn't reply. He shouted, "Aye, aye, sir," in response to the call of a ship's officer and hurried away.

Left to herself, Eliza wandered hopefully from deck to deck. She knew she would recognize Mr. Mercer if she could find him, but at the same time she wanted to avoid encountering Thankful Turner, who might remember her as the maidservant in the Endicott house.

She needn't have worried. Five minutes later she came upon Thankful face to face, but the young lady swept past without a glance. The gentry apparently never looked at servants. To the other passengers also, Eliza seemed quite invisible.

After an hour's fruitless attempt to locate Mr. Mercer, Eliza's courage ebbed along with her energy. Walking along the empty upper deck with an off-shore wind in her face and her stomach contracting with hunger pains, she came upon a canvas-covered lifeboat with a loose rope that seemed to offer temporary protection. Not so much on impulse as in quiet desperation, she managed to climb into the boat, pull the canvas back in place, then wriggle past the oarsmen's seats and curl up in a shivering ball with her head pillowed on her bundle of clothing. Too fatigued to care anymore, heedless of the consequences of capture, she soon fell asleep.

Two hours later, at midafternoon, Eliza was awakened suddenly by a triple blast on the ship's whistle. The sound, close to her, was earsplitting. She sat bolt upright, her head hitting the canvas cover of the lifeboat before she realized where she was.

A minute later she became aware that the steamer was under way. At the same instant a passing sailor, whose attention was attracted by her sudden movement, lifted the flapping corner of canvas and peered in at her with astonished blue eyes.

"Well, what the—?"

Eliza crawled forward, saw that the boy was fair-haired and young, with an open, pleasant face, and quickly put a finger to her lips. "Please!" she whispered.

The young man looked around cautiously, then bent closer. "Hey, look, I've got to report a stowaway."

A stowaway, so that's what I am, thought Eliza. A new crime to add to her growing list. "Please," she murmured again. "I'll go tell Mr. Mercer myself, as soon as I'm sure it's safe."

The deckhand hesitated. "You'll have a hard time finding him. He seems to have disappeared."

"Disappeared?" Eliza's heart fell.

"Don't worry. They say he's just in hiding until we drop anchor off Sandy Hook and the captain can sort out the passengers who haven't paid their fares."

"What will happen to them?" Eliza asked in a whisper.

"They'll be sent back aboard the tugboat, I suppose."

Eliza gasped. "You can't let that happen to me! I have nowhere to go."

The boy looked dubious. "Aw, come on now. What are you, an orphan?"

Eliza nodded miserably. "The asylum sent me out as a maidservant, but the lady didn't pay me anything at all for three years, so I ran away. *Please* don't tell on me!"

Still doubtful, the deckhand stared straight into Eliza's gray eyes. "Are you telling me the truth? Swear to it!"

Eliza crossed her heart. "I swear. Honestly."

With a sigh the young man glanced around again, then hastily made the flapping canvas fast. Eliza was alone and in the dark once more. "Get below, Harry, the old man's looking for you," she heard a voice say. Then steps receded. She heaved a sigh of relief and gratitude. Harry wouldn't give her away. She was sure of it. If only her luck would hold out!

Now that she was awake, Eliza became increasingly hungry. It was no wonder, for she had eaten nothing since breakfast yesterday morning. The thought of starving became almost as great a worry as the thought of being discovered and sent back to Salem in disgrace. For the moment, however, there was nothing she could do about food. She flexed her toes, chafed her cold hands, and thought about Harry's compassionate blue eyes. She was glad to know the sailor's name.

After a time the steamer slowed down. Eliza peeped out and saw land looming near at hand, then heard the long, heavy groan of an anchor chain being let out. There were shouts, footsteps, a good deal of calling back and forth from a tugboat lying alongside, angry voices raised in protest, and several unidentifiable thumps.

Eliza's curiosity overcame her good judgment, and she peeked under the canvas again. The lifeboat in which she was hiding seemed to be above and to the left of a ladder reaching down to the tug. Descending the ladder gingerly were an assorted group of people— several weeping girls, a middle-aged woman, and a gray-haired man with a wife and five children. Apparently all of them were being sent back to New York.

The disappointed passengers kept shouting, "Mr. Mercer! Mr. Mercer!" as they were herded along by the crew, but the leader of the expedition failed to appear.

Where, wondered Eliza, could Mr. Mercer be? Until that moment she hadn't realized how much she had counted on seeing his benign smile, the smile she remembered so well from the night he had dined with the Endicotts. Surely she could hope for his protection if she threw herself on his mercy. (He had seemed like such a nice man.) Yet the fate of the people huddled on the tugboat in the January dusk sent a chill of apprehension down her spine.

Chapter 4

As the tugboat chugged back toward New York's harbor, the *Continental* hauled anchor and put out to sea. When darkness thickened, Harry appeared to tell the stowaway that it was safe to come out now—if ever—because she could no longer be sent home.

Eliza straightened from her cramped position and emerged as quickly as possible from the lifeboat. Quickly Harry retied the canvas. "You never seen me, hear?"

"I understand. And thank you!" Eliza looked up into the young man's clear eyes, noted the kindliness of his expression, and spoke from the depths of her heart. She straightened her skirts, vainly tried to smooth her hair, and with misgiving watched Harry walk away. The time had come to find Mr. Mercer, even though his compassion could no longer be counted on.

The lighthouse at Sandy Hook had disappeared in the distance when Eliza made her way down from the boat deck. Drawn by the sound of voices, she entered the warmth of a crowded saloon. Confusion was as great as ever. Girls were gathered in clusters around an occasional dark-suited man. Uniformed officers were trying to answer passengers' questions while a handful of children scampered to and fro, too excited to heed their parents' commands to stand still and be quiet. Eliza stopped uncertainly in the doorway, surprised at the number of married couples aboard. Mr. Mercer's plan to transport only young ladies must have gone awry.

Everyone was complaining. Apparently none of the promised repairs had been made to the steamer's fittings since its days as a troop transport. The galley was in such a state that the cook, distinguishable by a tall chef's hat, threw up his hands and bellowed that no meal could be served tonight. From scraps of conversation Eliza learned that nobody could find Mr. Mercer. His stateroom was empty, the captain hadn't seen him, and the officers were as mystified as most of the passengers.

"Where is he?"

"What's happened?"

"Our guiding star has disappeared!"

Edging into the room, Eliza stood against a wall unnoticed, listening to the remarks of the passengers nearest her. Nobody glanced her way. Again she had the strange sensation of being invisible.

A commotion attracted her attention as a flushed and laughing young lady began to inch through the throng, followed by a couple of deckhands. With an air of knowing what she was about she ordered the forward hatch to be raised. Eliza crowded close with the rest, and the girl hallooed down the dark hole. "It's safe to come up now!"

The onlookers were rewarded by the sight of their grimy but impenitent leader emerging from the coal bin. His red hair had turned a mousy gray, and his beard was sprinkled with a black powder. "There was no use trying to face it out," he explained with a shake of his head that engulfed him in a cloud. "My resources are limited." To Eliza, Mr. Mercer looked undignified and sheepish. His face was sooty and his eyes had lost their pious glow. More than ever she shrank from approaching him.

As matters turned out, she didn't have to. Among the girls and women surrounding the open hatch Eliza's childish figure, in a short dress and threadbare orphanage coat, was as conspicuous to Mr. Mercer as a tattered Cinderella at a ball. "Where did you come from?" he asked in a voice hoarsened by coal dust. "You don't belong on board!"

The nearby passengers no longer seemed to find Eliza invisible and turned to stare at her, while those farther away craned their necks in the direction of Mr. Mercer's accusing finger. "I—I—" stammered Eliza, but she was too shy and too terrified to go on.

Mr. Mercer moved a pace closer, his brows drawn together in an angry frown. "Answer me!" he barked.

Eliza swallowed hard and managed to find her voice. "I came from Salem," she said in a whisper. "From the Endicotts'."

"The Endicotts?" Mr. Mercer made an obvious effort to recall the name, but shook his head impatiently.

"I was the housemaid there when you came to dinner."

"The housemaid?" Mr. Mercer's voice rose as if he found the word distasteful.

Eliza nodded. "I dropped the crystal bowl. Remember?" she asked naively, thinking that an accident of such major proportion might jog the gentleman's memory.

Mr. Mercer bowed his head and held it with both soot-blackened hands. "Oh, my God," he intoned in a distinctly unclerical manner.

Eliza gulped, but knew that she must gather courage to explain. "You spoke so forcefully of a girl's opportunities in Seattle," she said in her whispering voice. "I was sure you'd be good to me."

"My God!" said Mr. Mercer again.

There was a titter from the young ladies within earshot, a light, teasing flutter of laughter that served to alert Mr. Mercer not only to his unprepossessing appearance but also to his obligations. "If you will excuse me," he said with more ceremony than the occasion seemed to warrant, "I will rejoin you when I have cleaned up a bit."

Ignoring Eliza, along with the rest of his audience, he marched away with a careful dignity, presumably heading for his stateroom. The deckhands dropped the hatch cover with a bang, and the girls at once became hilarious.

"Can you imagine?"

"Isn't he a card?"

"A man of the cloth. Who is he kidding?"

"He's a scoundrel. That's what he is!"

The last remark came from a coarse-looking young woman with rouged cheeks and auburn ringlets on her forehead. Her wide-set green eyes were mischievous, her grin merry. "A churchman," she mused. "Well, we'll see what we shall see!"

"The trip is just beginning," murmured another bystander. "We'd better try—all of us—to get along."

The young woman, who was called Rosie, turned away with a shrug and fastened her eyes on Eliza. "How were you smuggled aboard, dearie? And how old are you anyway?"

Eliza ignored the first question. "I'm going on sixteen," she replied. Then, seizing the opportunity, she added quickly, "I'm aiming to work for my passage by doing laundry." She glanced around at the others with a timid but hopeful expression. "I've been trained as a laundress," she said, only slightly stretching the truth.

"What do you charge?" Rosie asked playfully.

"I—I don't know." Eliza stumbled, quite unprepared to set a price on her services. "What do you think is right?"

"I'll give you a dollar a week until I run out of money," suggested Rosie with a certain bravado, "but you must do my bed sheets as well as my clothes."

"A dollar a week's too much," objected a thrifty matron, holding a small boy by the hand.

"You set your rates; I'll set mine," said Rosie

rudely. Then she winked at Eliza. "Don't sell your-self cheap," she advised.

A tall, bespectacled young man inched through a clutter of crinolines. Unbearded, his face was so thin and sallow that Eliza wondered if he were ill. "Do you know how to iron shirts, miss?"

"I'm more used to ladies' clothes," Eliza confessed, "but I'll be glad to try."

The young man nodded politely. "My name is Alexander Stenn. I'm in Stateroom 13." He looked as if he'd like to ask another question, but apparently thought better of it. After considering her curiously for a moment or two, he turned away.

Thirteen. An unlucky number, but no matter, thought Eliza. Her spirits began to lift as it became evident she would not be unemployed during the voyage. That is, if anyone could provide her with an iron!

The crowd of passengers was shifting and regroup-ing. Many were complaining of being hungry, and someone persuaded the cook to send tea and biscuits to the saloon. His efforts seemed to suit nobody but Eliza, who wolfed the biscuits ravenously and swal-lowed the scalding tea with an appreciation only real hunger could generate.

In half an hour Mr. Mercer reappeared, washed and combed, his clerical demeanor reestablished. He moved among the passengers pompously, consoling some who were already homesick, encouraging others, and suggesting that everyone go to bed early, since the weather was turning stormy and cold.

Where could she sleep? Eliza dared not approach Mr. Mercer. She watched the young women drift away in twos and threes, until finally Rosie took pity on her.

"I'm bunking with an old maid and a proper pill, but there's a pipe berth in our cabin. It must be left over from the troopship. You're welcome to climb up to it if you like."

Eliza's heart leaped. "But what about your roommate?"

Rosie's eyes twinkled. "Miss Drummond's going out as a missionary to the Indians. Let's see if she'll show a little Christian charity."

Rosie's blowsiness, decided Eliza thankfully, concealed a kind heart. Trotting along in her benefactor's wake, she tried to express her gratitude.

"Wait'll you see the pipe berth," Rosie cautioned. "It won't be no bed of roses, dearie."

The pipe berth, in fact, looked both fragile and fearsome, a string hammock swung between two pipes fastened to the stateroom's ceiling. Miss Drummond, whose graying hair was worn in a prim bun, was on her knees beside her bunk when the pair entered. "Saying her prayers," Rosie explained needlessly to Eliza. "It's bound to take awhile."

Yawning, Rosie slipped out of her dress, hung it on a hook, loosened the laces of her corset, and flopped down on her bed with a sigh of relief. "Time enough to hunt through my luggage tomorrow," she said lazily. "Tonight I'll sleep as I am."

Eliza tossed her bundle-handkerchief up to the pipe

berth, folding her coat and dress and stashing them away in a corner. Then she climbed a ladder to the swinging hammock while Miss Drummond continued her prayers. Whether Rosie's roommate was indignant at the arrival of a third person was not to be learned that evening. Eliza fell asleep before Miss Drummond arose from her knees, and not until dawn the next day did she open her eyes.

A gong sounded for breakfast at seven o'clock, and the passengers, more than a hundred in all but far fewer than Mr. Mercer had counted on, hurried to see what the cook had managed to produce. The married couples clustered together, far outnumbered by the girls, who had already begun to sort themselves into cliques. The few single men looked wary on this first morning at sea and sat together at the far end of one of the long tables. Mr. Mercer breakfasted with Captain Windsor and the senior officers, as he apparently considered his prerogative.

Eliza slipped into an empty seat as far from the captain's table as possible. Excited young women, refreshed by the night's sleep, talked and laughed across her, making acquaintances, learning each other's names, discussing the single men on board, one of whom (it was stated on good authority) was a reporter from the *New York Times*.

"You'd better behave, Rosie," someone called down the table, "else you're apt to get your name in the paper."

Everybody teased Rosie, who tossed her auburn curls and laughed good-naturedly. Like the rest, she was relieved to be away at last, away from the crowded city, and bound on high adventure to a fresh and unspoiled part of the land.

The state of euphoria lasted only a short time. By midmorning a chopping wind roiled the gray water and a heavy cross sea made the ship roll sickeningly. By sundown only a few passengers remained upright and able to contemplate the prospect of food. One of them was Eliza, who found to her surprise that she was not subject to seasickness, even though dishes and furniture seemed to be seized with the contagion, swooping here and there while they rattled and clattered alarmingly.

The cook had an easy night of it. He served the captain's table, including Mr. Mercer, then sent food to the other survivors: Mr. Roger Conant, the *New York Times* reporter, Mr. Stenn, whose shirts needed laundering, a couple of sturdy children accompanied by their mother, a vivacious girl named Sally Marshall, and Eliza herself.

A waiter staggered to and fro with a tray held high on the palm of one hand, balanced precariously against the pitching of the ship, while the men talked about the foul weather and about the anguish of the young ladies whom Mr. Conant referred to as the "virgins."

"Some of them are positively frantic," he reported. "Not only are they seasick; they're convinced that the ship will sink."

"Will it?" asked one of the children, who sounded more excited than scared.

"I don't think so," Mr. Conant replied with a smile.

"Captain Windsor is said to be a splendid seaman. He earned a fine reputation with the Navy during the war."

Eliza glanced around at the captain, a well-knit, aging man, gray-haired and gray-eyed, who carried himself with dignity. Neither his wife nor daughter, who were accompanying him on the voyage, had appeared this evening. Even Mr. Mercer was beginning to look a little queasy and refused the meat course after he had finished his soup.

"Were you in the war, Mr. Stenn?" asked Sally Marshall from across the table.

"No, ma'am. I was in school."

"College, he means," said Mr. Conant smoothly.

"Oh, my goodness!" Miss Marshall sounded superficially impressed. "Are you a Harvard man?"

Mr. Stenn flushed, and Eliza suspected he was embarrassed by so much attention. "No, ma'am," he said shyly. "I went to Columbia."

"A fine university," said Mr. Conant, "which numbers Alexander Hamilton, John Jay, and a score of other famous men among its graduates."

"Really?" murmured Miss Marshall. "And why are you heading west, Mr. Stenn? To teach?"

The young man nodded, and Eliza noticed that, for the first time, his eyes contained a sparkle when he replied, "It has been my fondest dream!"

Having cleared the dinner plates, the waiter created a diversion by skidding across the floor with the dessert dishes and landing almost in Eliza's lap. The children laughed uproariously, their mother said,

"Sh!" and Mr. Conant leaned forward and spoke pleasantly. "I don't think I know your name."

"Eliza Foster, sir." From ingrained habit, Eliza spoke as a servant would to a gentleman.

"You must be one of the youngest of Mr. Mercer's virgins."

Delighted to be thought in any manner attached to the Mercer girls, Eliza said, "Perhaps, but I'm older than I look. I'll be sixteen next month." Obviously the *New York Times* reporter could not have been present at the confrontation near the coal hatch, and she felt rather relieved.

Mr. Conant grinned. "Sixteen! That makes Asa Mercer and me old men. I'm past thirty, not like Alex here."

Eliza glanced at Mr. Stenn, quite unable to guess his age. He still looked pale and sickly, coughing from time to time and brushing a hand over a cowlick that kept his soft brown hair from lying properly flat. "Youth isn't everything," he said with an apologetic smile, then took off his spectacles to polish them on a corner of his napkin. "You are a man of experience, while I am on my way to my first real job."

Mr. Conant smiled deprecatingly. "Lucky fellow! The world before you," he said teasingly. "I quite envy you."

"And I you," said Mr. Stenn. "It must be splendid to be a writer." He sounded polite and admiring but not really envious at all. A few minutes earlier, when he had spoken of teaching, the expression in his eyes had been quite different, full of enthusiasm and anticipation. Now he was saying what was expected of him, not speaking from his heart.

The remarks that followed were quite above Eliza's head, because the two men began to discuss writing as a career. She sat very still and listened carefully, although Miss Marshall began to yawn behind her hand. How marvelous to be here at all, Eliza thought. How astonishing to be seated at the same table with a man of the world like Mr. Conant, sophisticated, sure of himself, and working for the most famous newspaper in the United States.

Mr. Stenn she could not judge. He had clear hazel eyes and a fine-skinned, beardless face. With his glasses off he had seemed quite young. Now he looked less diffident, but very serious, almost owlish. Sally Marshall yawned again, obviously bored by the conversation between the two men, and after a moment she excused herself and pushed back her chair.

Hoping to escape from the saloon before Mr. Mercer managed to accost her, Eliza followed suit. Unfortunately, she was a few seconds too late. As she gained the corridor Mr. Mercer called, from right behind her, "Young woman, I want to speak to you!"

Eliza quailed, but she turned and waited, trying desperately not to look as frightened as she felt. Mr. Mercer, with his beetling brows and penetrating eyes, seemed to bear no resemblance to the kindly man who had sat at the Endicotts' dinner table. He said sternly, "You know, of course, that stowing aboard ship is a criminal offense."

"I didn't intend to stay aboard without your permission, sir," Eliza replied meekly. "I couldn't find you. I looked everywhere!"

Roger Conant and Alexander Stenn came through the door just in time to hear this last remark. Amusement flickered in the reporter's eyes. "As did a good many other people," he said quite audibly.

Mr. Mercer ignored this jibe and fixed his glance firmly on Eliza. "Passage aboard this ship costs two hundred dollars. How much are you prepared to pay?" He put out a hand to steady himself against the corridor wall, inadvertently barring the other two men from passing. "Answer me!" he ordered.

"Nothing, sir, right now. But I'll give you the money I earn doing laundry for the passengers." Eliza added, with sudden inspiration, "And, of course, I'll do yours free."

Although this suggestion didn't amuse Mr. Mercer, Alexander Stenn smiled and Roger Conant chuckled. "That's quite an offer," he said, "but wouldn't it be only fair to let the child keep a few dollars to help her get started in a strange town?"

At this point Mr. Stenn tried to edge past. He looked uncomfortable and obviously wished to stay clear of this dispute between a servant girl and the expedition's leader. Another lurch of the ship threw Eliza against him, however, and he put out an arm to steady her, then remained standing by awkwardly.

Eliza didn't appreciate Mr. Conant's intervention. She was tired of being called a child and determined to make an effort to stand on her own two feet. Gathering more courage than she had shown since running away from the Endicotts', she stared at the floor and said stiffly, "I think this is a matter between Mr. Mercer and myself."

Curiously, this statement seemed to mollify the expedition's leader. "Since I, and not Mr. Conant, am saddled with your presence on this ship, I can't but agree with you, Eliza. Each week you may bring me an accounting of the money you've earned. I suppose you can add and subtract?"

Mr. Mercer's tone was patronizing, the question clearly intended to embarrass her. "I can do arithmetic," Eliza said.

"I shall keep a record of what you are able to pay on account," Mr. Mercer continued. "At the end of the voyage we will look to the future."

Weak with relief—she would be tolerated, if not welcomed—Eliza agreed to these terms. When Mr. Mercer went back to the saloon and Mr. Conant turned to talk to one of the ship's officers, she would have gone on down the corridor, except that Mr. Stenn was standing in her way.

He looked at her with a vaguely troubled expression, cleared his throat, then said, "If I may make a suggestion—"

"Yes?"

"I should be very careful of making any promises to Mr. Mercer. Any promises at all. Once he's sure he has you under his thumb, I'm afraid he'll never let up on you."

The advice was kindly enough, and Eliza suspected that Mr. Stenn's prediction was right, but behind the actual words he had a manner of speaking she knew well—the manner of a gentleman addressing a servant. He was a university graduate, she was a housemaid. A *former* housemaid, she told herself sternly, and her chin lifted. Surprisingly, she found herself saying, "I am no longer a bond servant, Mr. Stenn. I shall do what I think right with the money I earn."

Looking abashed, the young man stepped aside to let Eliza pass. "I had no intention—" he started, then broke off. "I was just trying—" The attempted apology was not acknowledged. Having made an astonishing show of independence, Eliza was hurrying off in the direction of her stateroom.

Dignity, which seemed to be called for under the circumstances, was impossible to maintain, however. As the ship rocked and rolled Eliza staggered from side to side of the long corridor, holding herself upright with difficulty and bruising her shoulders in the process. The storm was getting worse.

She gained the door, wrenched it open, and lurched into the fetid cubicle where she found Miss Drummond and Rosie in great distress. They were crouched on their berths, holding their stomachs and groaning. Both had been very, very sick.

"You need some fresh air," Eliza said, trying to hold her breath as she edged over to open the porthole. A cold, reviving wind was almost immediately followed by a flood of water, drenching Miss Drummond's berth and provoking a tirade. "Now look what you've done! Lord, help me! Oh, my, why did I ever agree to emigrate?" Her graying hair had fallen from its pins and was streaming down her back, her face was ashen, and her stomach continued to heave. She clutched a basin in her lap as she mingled prayers with castigation.

"Oh, for God's sake, help me up on deck," Rosie begged, when she could make herself heard, but in spite of Eliza's determined efforts they could get no farther than the steps leading up from the passageway. Rosie sank down on the lowest tread, holding her head with her hands as her stomach heaved with every pitch of the ship. "I hope I die," she moaned.

"You don't hope anything of the kind. You'll feel better tomorrow," Eliza promised.

Rosie shook her head.

"Breathe deeply. At least, out here the air is fresh."

Rosie shook her head again.

Eliza stayed with her for half an hour, then struggled back to the stateroom and tried to clean up the mess. By now apparently nothing remained in the stomachs of either of her cabin mates, and by midnight she had persuaded Miss Drummond to lie flat on the stripped and turned mattress, while Rosie, who had been persuaded to totter back to bed, was curled on her side with her eyes closed.

The gale blew itself out in the night, and the next morning most of Mr. Mercer's young ladies managed to stand upright and head for the deck. There, bundled in the warmest wraps they owned, they sank weakly into chairs. After a while the cook sent up hot tea, and by noon more than half of them had recuperated sufficiently to appear for lunch.

Meanwhile, Eliza had been scurrying around the strange and rather frightening lower decks trying to discover the whereabouts of washtubs. The cook sent her to a steward, who passed her along to a grizzled old sailor, who took a key from a rack and opened the door to a dank and airless laundry room with two standing tubs. There was hot and cold running water, a welcome boon, and a couple of buckets filled with hard chunks of yellow soap that smelled of lye.

"I'm planning to do washing and ironing for some of the passengers," Eliza told the sailor diffidently. "Must I get permission to use all this?" Her glance included the tubs, a worn wicker laundry basket, and the pails full of soap.

"Who's to stop you? Here, I'll give you the key, but mind you take good care of it."

"Thank you. Thank you very much!" Eliza's gratitude shone in her eyes, although her manner was self-effacing.

The old man grinned, showing tobacco-stained teeth. "From what I hear about the conditions topside, you'll have your work cut out for you."

Eliza's services were indeed in great demand. She was glad her stomach was strong as she washed sheets and garments reeking of vomit and carried them up to the hurricane deck, where she rigged up a line and hung them in the air to dry. Besides the clothesline, tossed in a corner of the laundry, she had also unearthed a box of sturdy wooden clothespins. She was in business, and her bewilderment was lessening. She was glad she had dared to run away, glad she had managed to escape detection until the ship was well out to sea. Somehow, from now on, she was sure she could muddle through.

The sun came out in the early afternoon, the ocean calmed down, and Mrs. Windsor, the captain's wife, walked about the boat deck assuring everyone that they would soon move into warmer waters and had little more to fear.

Toward sunset, as she was carrying a last basket of clothes to be hung in the breeze, Eliza came on Harry polishing brass. His smile of greeting was warm and friendly. "So Mr. Mercer didn't throw you overboard!"

Eliza liked the blue-eyed sailor. "You can see I'm still here."

"How did you survive the storm?"

"Quite well. I don't seem to get seasick."

"You're lucky."

"I know."

The conversation might have reached a dead end, but as Eliza started to pin whipping sheets to the line Harry walked over and leaned against the smokestack. "I've been thinking about you a lot," he said.

Eliza's heartbeat quickened. Nobody had ever spoken to her in this fashion. She flushed but didn't meet the sailor's glance.

"What are you going to do when you reach Washington Territory?" he asked after a pause.

"Look for a place as a housemaid, I suppose. That's all I know."

"San Francisco's a pretty good town," said Harry after another moment or two. "That's where I live."

Eliza had no notion of coquetry. She turned thoughtful, asking, "Could a girl find work there?"

"A girl can find work anywhere in the West." Harry spoke confidently, then added, "San Francisco's bigger than Seattle, much bigger." He seemed to take pride in the fact.

Again there was a long pause, broken by Eliza. "What is your last name, Harry?"

"Svenson. S-v-e-n-s-o-n."

"Norwegian?"

"Swedish. But I was born over here."

"Mr. Svenson, are you married?" Eliza dared to ask.

Harry threw back his head and roared with laughter. "I'll say not. And won't be till I've turned twenty and find me a likely girl!"

Innocently Eliza asked, "Are you looking for a bride?"

"Isn't every fellow my age?" Harry asked. "But I don't want none of your fancy young ladies in crinolines. I want a sensible girl who won't run wild when I go to sea." He stared down at the rag and can of polish he held in his hand. "A girl who's a good housewife, like my ma."

"Is that all?"

"What do you mean, all?"

"Aren't you interested in finding a girl you can—love?"

"Sure. Why not?" Harry seemed embarrassed. He

went back to rubbing the metalwork, but turned his head to say, "I'm not much on sweet talk, though."

"That doesn't matter," said Eliza reassuringly. "It's how you feel that counts." She gathered up the basket of laundry already dry and smiled to herself as she started off to distribute it below.

Chapter 5

On the first Sunday morning at sea Mr. Mercer decided to hold religious services in the saloon. Promptly at eleven o'clock a gong was rung to summon members of his expedition to worship.

The saloon was crowded when Eliza slipped through the door behind the rest. Increasingly aware of her ambiguous position on board—neither a hired servant nor a paid-up passenger—she did not presume (as Mrs. Endicott would have put it) to mingle with those who were more fortunate.

Nor did loneliness trouble her as she was accustomed to being alone. Naturally shy, she had made few friends at the orphanage, and in the past three years there had been no opportunity to seek companionship. The house on Chestnut Street was virtually a prison without bars.

The last seat in the saloon had been taken, but Eliza didn't mind. She stood with a few other stragglers at the back of the congregation while Mr. Mercer ex-

plained that the hymn singing this morning would be
without accompaniment, since the piano brought
aboard had not yet been set up on legs.

This information was quite obvious to everyone.
The piano body had been skittering dangerously across
the saloon all during the storm, and quite a few of the
girls nursed barked shins as a consequence. After some
feeble off-key singing of more or less familiar stanzas,
Mr. Mercer said a prayer for the vessel's safety at sea
and its propitious arrival in the West. Eliza bowed her
head politely and marveled that this astonishing man
could change color with the ease of a chameleon. This
morning he was bathed in a deep religious glow. Yesterday he had been coldly stern. At the Endicotts' dinner table he had been intrepid and smiling, filled with
great plans. Perhaps he was the hypocrite Rosie
thought him.

The hymn singing over, Mr. Mercer took a newspaper clipping from the pocket of his dark suit and
read a sermon that he credited to Henry Ward Beecher
of the Plymouth Church in Brooklyn. Eliza found Mr.
Beecher's remarks keen and frankly humorous. No
Salem clergyman had ever dared be so entertaining,
at least not while she and the other orphans were
seated sedately in the balcony of the Episcopal Church.

After Mr. Mercer had folded his paper and offered
a benediction, most of the passengers repaired to the
deck to await the bell that would signal the next meal.
Eliza, standing alone by the rail, noticed that the girls
were quickly settling into a routine. Recovered from
their indisposition and accustomed, by now, to the

rolling of the steamer, the prettier ones had struck up an acquaintance with the younger officers. Thankful Turner, animated and pink cheeked, was promenading this morning with the third engineer. The plainer girls clustered together or occupied themselves with needlework, and one serious-minded lady was intent on plans to start a small school for the ten children aboard. She obtained permission from Captain Windsor to use one of the lifeboats as a classroom and scurried about for the rest of the day recruiting pupils for her weekly classes in geography, reading, writing, and arithmetic.

Whenever Eliza wasn't working over a washtub, she fell into the habit of dropping by to listen to the teacher, a wisp of a woman named Harriet Stevens. "How far did you get in school?" Miss Stevens asked Eliza one day.

"Just past sixth grade."

"Then you've studied the subjects I'm teaching."

"Yes," Eliza admitted, without trying to explain that it was fun to refresh her memory. Instead, she said, "I wish I could have gone on."

"Do you like to read?" Miss Stevens asked with directness.

Eliza nodded quickly.

"There's supposed to be a library aboard, donated by an altruistic New Yorker named Peter Cooper, but the books haven't been unpacked yet. I'll see if I can hurry things along."

Eventually Miss Stevens was successful. After the piano was set up on its legs, the library books were found and unpacked. Mr. Mercer, in a high-handed manner, appropriated the matched sets, which he considered the most valuable, and the rest were placed on shelves in the saloon. As soon as possible, Miss Stevens brought Eliza a copy of *Jane Eyre*, then "for contrast," she suggested *The Three Musketeers*. A ready pupil, Eliza was introduced to the fascination of the novel and spent hours with her nose in a book.

As the weather became milder, however, free time was at a premium. The young ladies brought out lighter clothes, washable cottons that required long hours of ironing. Sensing an advantage, Mr. Mercer had unearthed two flatirons, and Eliza found herself busy for most of the daylight hours.

She washed in the mornings, then took things up to dry in the sun, looking forward to her meetings with Harry, who somehow contrived to be occupied nearby when she appeared. His face would light up with pleasure when he spotted her, and as their friendship ripened they began to explore each other's past.

Harry told Eliza all about San Francisco, which he predicted would become a huge and exciting city one of these days. In return, Eliza tried to describe Salem, the handsome little seaport town with brick sidewalks and cobbled streets. She told Harry about the Endicott house, with its fine furniture and beautiful objects brought back by the China traders of a century ago. She dwelt on the shell collection it was her duty to dust, but she didn't say anything about Mrs. Endicott or Amelia. Her memories of them were too bitter to share with anyone.

On an especially balmy morning Rosie came upon Eliza and Harry standing close together in the lee of a line of laundry. She winked impishly at Eliza and that night called up to the pipe berth, "So you've found yourself a young man!"

The remark caught Eliza by surprise. She could feel herself flush in the darkness and stammered absurdly, "What young man?"

"Don't be coy, Eliza!" chided Rosie, as Miss Drummond turned on her side with her face toward the wall. "Anyone can see with half an eye that you've made a hit with that good-looking sailor boy. As sure as my name's Rosie Brennan you've got yourself a beau."

Eliza collected herself and replied more sharply than necessary, "Stop talking nonsense, Rosie! Harry's a nice lad, and he has been very kind to me, but there's nothing between us. Nothing at all."

"You'd better keep it that way," Miss Drummond advised unexpectedly. "Mr. Mercer's dead set against any of his party getting familiar with the officers or crew."

"Mr. Mercer better not get too picky," parried Rosie. "We're not a bunch of nuns."

The interchange quickly ended, but Eliza lay awake for an hour, thinking about Harry and wondering whether Rosie showed a certain discernment. It was true that Harry regularly sought her out, and it was also true that he paid her occasional compliments, often clumsy but rather appealing. Sometimes Harry seemed almost as young and inexperienced as she was herself. What if Rosie were right, and he was romantically interested? The possibility was a heartwarming one to contemplate.

Although many of the girls in the expedition spent long hours before their stateroom mirrors, arranging their hair, pinching their cheeks to redden them becomingly, adjusting their corsets, and appraising their images, Eliza had never taken time to wonder if she was attractive. Her clothes were so poor, her station in life so lowly, that the thought of marriage rarely had entered her head. Yet she knew that Amelia Endicott thought of little else, and apparently Thankful Turner was also out to catch a husband. Thankful was so pretty, so fashionable and imperious, swinging a little purse from a delicate wrist as she paraded the deck with her latest conquest, that every man on board glanced after her appreciatively.

Alexander Stenn's admiration was particularly transparent. He engaged Thankful in conversation at every opportunity and was not in the least daunted when she either teased or ignored him, then walked off with a gentleman more to her taste.

Eliza suspected, however, that Thankful's flirtations on shipboard were merely practice for the opportunities that would present themselves in Seattle. No wonder Mr. Mercer was doing his best to keep the girls from toying with the affections of the officers. He was bound to protect the cargo of brides he was carrying west on the *Continental*. That she, Eliza Foster, might be one of them seemed unlikely, however. Swaying there in her hammock, no more than half awake now, she allowed her thoughts to rove. What did she know about Washington Territory, after all? And Harry made San Francisco sound busy and booming and very attractive indeed.

The next morning Eliza studied her reflection in the mirror with more than cursory interest. In the fortnight aboard ship her face had lost its pinched look and her eyes had acquired sparkle. The other girls complained about the monotony of the food and the abrasive wind that burned their lips and coarsened their skins, but Eliza had never been so happy, so well fed, or so free. She worked hard, charged a good price for her services, and was able to give two or three dollars a week to Mr. Mercer. Life looked actually promising!

And Harry's attentions were like the icing on the cake. When he described Seattle (which he had never seen) as a raw settlement of shacks and muddy roads carved out of the wilderness, Eliza listened attentively. He painted San Francisco in livelier hues, discounting reports of its vice, repeatedly predicting a golden future. Then he suggested shyly, "I'd like you to meet my ma and pa if you stop off there. The cruise ends in Frisco anyway, and you'll have to go on to Seattle by bark, so you wouldn't be losing no time."

Eliza was so surprised that she reacted to this information rather than to Harry's invitation. "You mean the *Continental* doesn't take us all the way? I don't think Mr. Mercer has made that clear."

Harry grinned. "He'll be forced to when the time

comes. And I'll make a bet that a good many of his young ladies will stay in California. It's a good deal more civilized than Oregon or Washington."

"You should be a salesman, not a sailor, Harry."

"And spend my days on city streets or indoors? Not likely!" Harry glanced at the steamer's wake and said, "This is where I belong, and this is where I'll earn my bread and butter, aboard ship."

Eliza admired such commitment, but she was impelled to ask, "What are your ambitions, Harry?"

"Ambitions?"

"Why, yes. You don't want to remain a deckhand, surely?"

Harry looked puzzled. "It takes brains and pull to work your way up," he said slowly. "And you've got to get in right with the officers."

"Aren't you in right?"

Harry hesitated. "With most I get along, but I'm having a bit of trouble with the first mate, Mr. Corrigan."

"Has he seen you talking with me when you should be working?"

"No. It goes deeper than that. Oh, forget it," Harry said. "It's not important." He walked off with the can of paint he was carrying, and Eliza finished hanging up clothes, then went below to tidy herself for lunch.

On the way down she met Thankful Turner head on, and for the first time Miss Turner showed a sign of recognition. "I've seen you somewhere before we came aboard," she said. "Do you come from Salem?"

"Yes," said Eliza.

"Then why didn't you tell me straight off, when you came to fetch my laundry?"

"It wasn't my place to."

Thankful frowned, forgetting that it was unwise to wrinkle her creamy brow. Her eyes ran over Eliza's shabby dress. "Are you an orphan?"

"Yes," Eliza said again.

"From the asylum?"

Eliza nodded.

"I could have seen you in church—but no, I don't think so. Where did you work after you left the orphanage?"

Trapped, Eliza had to confess. "At the Endicotts'. I used to answer the door when you came to see Miss Amelia."

"Of course!" Thankful laughed reminiscently, in the high, clear treble that so enchanted not only Alexander Stenn but most of the other men. "Poor Amelia. She wanted so much to come along, but of course her mother wouldn't hear of it."

"I know," whispered Eliza, wishing she could end this confrontation. Unfortunately, there was no way of slipping past Thankful's wired skirt, which completely blocked the narrow stairs.

The two stood facing each other for a long moment, Thankful assured and graceful, with a fetching dimple and a sagacious eye, Eliza throbbing with trepidation. Suppose Thankful wrote home and gave her away?

"How did you manage to escape?" The question was

put indolently, the tone far from severe, yet Eliza mistrusted Thankful.

Swallowing hard, she admitted, "I ran away."

"Did you?" Again there was a long pause. Then Thankful said, "I'm surprised you had that much spirit."

"Really?" Her indignation finally aroused, Eliza tossed caution to the wind sweeping down from the deck. "Why should you be surprised?"

Thankful shrugged.

Her voice lifting along with her chin, Eliza said, "You know nothing about me, Miss Turner. You have seen me—even spoken to me—dozens of times, but you don't know me at all."

Holding her laundry basket high, Eliza waited while Thankful backed down the two steps she had climbed and stood aside to let her pass. Back in the stateroom, Rosie, who was lolling on her berth, appeared not to notice Eliza's trembling as her momentary courage was supplanted by a growing fear. A few well-chosen words to Mrs. Turner, passed on within hours to Mrs. Endicott, the police alerted, telegrams sent or letters quickly written, and Eliza could imagine herself being dragged off the *Continental* at the first possible port.

She wanted to confide in Rosie, but she was so accustomed to keeping her own counsel that she couldn't bring herself to bare her secret. Instead, trying to regain self-control, she dumped the laundry basket in the corner and unbraided her hair, brushing it as Rosie watched her. *I shouldn't have been so bold,*

Eliza thought. I shouldn't have talked back. However, although surprised at her own temerity, she wasn't entirely sorry. I'm not the frightened little mouse who scampered through Salem more than a fortnight ago, she said to herself. I'm not the same girl at all!

After a while Rosie said idly, "You've got nice hair, Eliza, when it's loose like that." She twisted a finger around one of her own curls. "Why do you wear it in braids?"

"I don't know. I always have. Until lately I wore pigtails."

There was a discreet knock on the stateroom door, which Eliza answered, hairbrush in hand. She was used to people coming by with their laundry. Today Alexander Stenn stood outside, a bundle of soiled clothing in his arms.

"I was looking for Eliza." he said.

"I'm Eliza."

Mr. Stenn was clearly taken aback. "Excuse me. You look different, with your hair down."

Eliza reached for the bundle. Again she sensed something patronizing in his manner, although she felt sorry for him. As Rosie pointed out, he was making a bit of a fool of himself over Thankful, who could be seen trying to avoid his attentions without being actually rude. "He might as well give up chasing that dolly-bird," was Rosie's conclusion. "Miss Turner has an eye out for bigger game."

Once the door was closed behind the customer, Rosie took up her interrupted conversation with Eliza. "When I was your age," she said, "I always tried to look older than I was. Now I try to look younger than I am."

She sounded so wistful that Eliza said, "You look fine to me."

"That's nice of you to say, but the question is, Why don't I look fine to the purser? You know him, don't you? Such a pretty man."

"The one with the smelly dog?"

"That's the one." Rosie sighed.

Everybody on board, with the exception of Rosie, disliked the big mongrel who slept most of the day under a table in the purser's office. To curry favor, Rosie began to take the dog on turns around the deck and even brought him tidbits from the table, but her attentions did not endear her to the dog's owner, who had the improbable name of Washington Debro. He remained determinedly aloof.

Rosie indulged in various ploys. She produced an autograph book, persuaded Mr. Conant to write in it, then on the strength of his signature affixed to some lines of trite verse, took the little book to Mr. Debro and presented him with a gold pen borrowed from the *Times* reporter. "You can keep it if you'll give me your autograph," she wheedled shamelessly.

Mr. Debro, whose eye had been taken by a younger and more innocent girl, refused both the invitation and the gift, but Rosie's enthusiasm was hard to quench. Let the others flirt with whom they liked. Her attachment to the purser remained firm.

Firm, that is, until the weather turned truly mild. Then, not to Eliza's surprise, Rosie abandoned Mr.

Debro as a lost cause. The dog wagged his tail and
begged to be walked whenever his former friend appeared, but Rosie took no further notice of him. She
didn't intend to spend these moonlit evenings pining
in her room while most of the men on board, officers
and passengers alike, were strolling on deck with their
arms around the waist of a pretty girl.

A few young ladies in the expedition had strong
feelings of delicacy that drew the line at such famil-
iarity, but Eliza noticed that they were the ones who
received little or no attention from the men.

Miss Drummond and Miss Stevens were among
those without escorts, as was a grieving widow who
intended to become an independent dressmaker. In
this group there was open disapproval of Rosie Brennan's behavior. She was bold, she was brash, she was
painted like a you-know-what, and the ladies literally
drew aside their skirts when she passed their deck
chairs. Eliza caught scraps of the conversation, and the
comments troubled her. She wanted to rush to Rosie's
defense, but of course she couldn't. All she could do
was ignore the slanderous tongues and remain firmly
loyal to her first real friend.

As the philandering prospered, Mr. Mercer took to
lecturing his flock on the importance of being modest
and virtuous. He repeated his rule forbidding the girls
to have any dealings with the officers, but to little effect.
Romances budded and even bloomed as the ship
steamed placidly through southern waters. Even Mr.
Mercer himself indulged in a brief escapade.

Suddenly struck by the charms of Sally Marshall,

who had become very friendly with Thankful, Mr. Mercer followed her up on deck on an evening when the moon was full. He found her flirting blithely with one of the engineers and went back to his stateroom to write a note commanding her to appear in the saloon the next morning.

Miss Marshall arrived ten minutes late and was told that every officer on board had designs on her. "If you give any of these men half a chance," stormed Mr. Mercer in his most pontifical tones, "it will certainly prove your ruin!"

Sally laughed in Mr. Mercer's face. "I'm quite able to take care of myself," she told him haughtily.

"I have forbidden you to consort with the officers, Miss Marshall!"

"I shall select my own company," she retorted.

"You dare refuse to take my advice?"

"Unless you care to refund my passage money," Sally said, "I will walk on deck with whomever I please, and I'd like to see you prevent me!"

News of this encounter spread quickly, and the young lady's show of temper especially delighted Rosie. She slapped her knee and roared with laughter. "That'll show the old man!"

Nearly all the girls started to refer to Mr. Mercer as the "old man," although someone had unearthed the information that he was only twenty-seven years of age. "What does it matter when he was born?" asked Rosie of everyone within earshot. "He acts as if he's ninety, with his sanctimonious airs."

On an evening when the moon was on the wane

Eliza met Harry up on the hurricane deck. "I have a little present for you," he had told her that morning. "Come up after dark, and I'll give it to you."

The invitation seemed nothing short of marvelous to Eliza. Although the weather was changing and the Atlantic was whipped with whitecaps, she didn't hesitate. At last, like the other girls, she had been asked to walk on deck with a young man!

The hurricane deck, however, offered little space for strolling. Obstacles interfered at every turn, smokestack, stanchions, the masts, the bridge. As the wind whipped in from the north, Eliza agreed to take shelter with Harry in the lifeboat where she had stowed away on the day the ship sailed.

She felt daring and rather apprehensive, but Harry helped her into the boat politely, then came to sit close beside her and talk in whispers. "We don't want to be discovered," he warned.

"Why? Is it against the rules?" Eliza asked.

"More or less."

More rather than less, Eliza suspected, and she wondered whether Harry's problems with the first mate, Mr. Corrigan, were worsening, but this moment was certainly no time to ask. Huddled under the canvas tarpaulin, she felt delightfully adventurous, and when Harry dared to hold her hand a thrill swept her, making her fingers tremble. Since Eliza had entered the asylum, no one had ever touched her tenderly. Indeed she could remember nobody, except Mrs. Endicott (who once had slapped her) ever touching her at all.

"I like you, Eliza," Harry said.

"I like you, too."

As an avowal of first love the exchange was far from passionate, but it was an avowal nevertheless. Instinctively Eliza felt that someday Harry would ask her to marry him, but she couldn't foresee her answer. She tried to imagine keeping house for a man who spent most of his life at sea, tried to envision the loneliness. But then she'd always been lonely. When she grew up a little more and came to know Harry better, perhaps she'd be able to accept the notion that many a girl had made a success of life with a seafaring man.

Love—romantic love—didn't occupy Eliza's thoughts. Although the reading of novels was opening a window on the world of emotions, her feelings were still dormant. Except that Eliza knew she liked Harry. She liked him a lot!

"What are you thinking about?" Harry asked.

"Nothing." Eliza quickly corrected herself. "That's not quite true. You, partly."

"I hope they're good thoughts."

"How could they be otherwise?" Eliza smiled in the darkness, and Harry squeezed her hand.

The pair sat in silence for a while, their shoulders touching, but Harry didn't try to "get fresh," as Rosie would have put it. Eliza was grateful. At this point holding hands was lovely, but quite enough.

In the sheltered nest of the lifeboat time seemed to stand still. The creaking of the mast, the slow throb of the engine, and the rising wind were all familiar noises, and therefore comforting. Harry, who was full of conversation in the daytime, talked little tonight. He seemed relaxed and happy, at peace with Eliza and his world.

Not until much later, when they had climbed out on deck again, did he say, "Aren't you interested in the present I promised you?"

Eliza, who had forgotten it, said, "Of course!"

"It isn't much, but since you seem to like seashells—" He pulled a curious necklace from his middy pocket and held it out.

"Shells?" The necklace was made of miniature tusks that glowed white in the darkness. When Eliza touched them, they felt like polished ivory.

"They're shells all right," Harry said. "The Indians in the Northwest used them for money in the old days."

"It's beautiful," Eliza breathed, examining the necklace in the moonlight. "Where ever did you get it?"

"I bought it from one of the crew," said Harry, pleased that she liked it.

Eliza slipped the chain of shells over her head and stroked it happily. Then, because she was truly touched, she leaned closer and put her head for a moment on Harry's shoulder. "Thank you very much indeed," she said softly. "Do you know, this is the first present I've ever had!"

Chapter 6

The expected tropical storm built up slowly the next day, thunderclouds forming and dissolving as the steamer rolled sturdily on toward the equator, which Mr. Mercer—after conferring with Captain Windsor—announced to be some 400 miles south.

At suppertime a number of girls decided to remain on deck rather than go below to the stuffy saloon, where for days they had been served nothing but fried salt beef, boiled beans, and tea steeped in salt water, a distasteful diet against which almost everyone rebelled.

Eliza, however, was hungry and ate with gusto, ignoring the grumbling of the other diners. "For the skinniest girl on board," called Mr. Conant down the length of the table, "you sure can put it away!"

Eliza wasn't offended. She grinned amiably, but had no time to make a reply, because at that moment there was a cry from a forward deck, a shout of alarm that brought the diners to their feet.

"Man overboard!" called voices from every side. "Man overboard!"

Out of the saloon in seconds, Captain Windsor was followed quickly by his officers. The passengers abandoned their unfinished dinners and crowded through the doors after them, tumbling over one another in their haste to reach the deck.

Rosie Brennan was among the first to get to the rail, Eliza among the last. Standing on tiptoe, she caught a glimpse of a life preserver floating on the waves.

"What happened?"

"Who is it?"

"One of the passengers?"

"They always say 'man overboard.' Could it be a girl?"

Questions came thick and fast, but nobody had the answers. As the ship's engine was throttled down the life preserver could be seen on the crest of a towering wave, where it teetered crazily for a moment before disappearing into a basin of black water on the far side.

"Can the fellow swim?"

"What are his chances?"

"Look, they're lowering a lifeboat!"

"In this sea?"

"Has the ship stopped then?"

"One blow from a blade of the screw—" A man's deep voice broke off in mid-sentence as he sliced a hand across his throat descriptively.

"Instant death," said the purser, sighing, "unless

the chap has enough presence of mind to strike clear of the ship."

"Aren't there sharks out there?" asked Thankful Turner with a shudder. She was looking queasy, but she didn't abandon her place by the rail.

Eliza said nothing. She watched the lifeboat pull away from the ship, surmounting a huge wave with difficulty, then falling into the deep trough that yawned beyond. The *Continental*'s engines were running again, and the ship turned laboriously and started to retrace its course.

Time crawled. Fifteen minutes passed, seeming like an hour, as the passengers strained to catch a glimpse of the lifeboat in the distance. No sunset lit up the sea tonight to help the search party. The angry storm clouds piled overhead had turned both water and sky dark and terrifying.

Nervously some of the passengers began to glance around, wondering if one of their number might indeed be missing.

"Who is it? Doesn't anyone know?"

"Where's Mr. Mercer? Maybe he's heard."

"Oh, the poor, poor man!" wept Thankful, leaning on the nearest male shoulder and dabbing at her brimming eyes with a small linen handkerchief.

Sally Marshall, made of sterner stuff, was inclined to be optimistic. She advised Thankful to save her tears. "They may rescue him yet."

"If he can swim against such waves," murmured Miss Drummond dismally.

"Perhaps he'll be able to float—"

Disconnected sections of sentences began to assail Eliza's ears like hailstones. She heard the ship's bell and automatically counted the strokes, although the sound seemed to come from a great distance. Then she looked up at the sky, aware that it was about to open any minute. The rain would come straight down in heavy curtains of water, blocking out all the visibility that was left.

After another endless quarter of an hour the lifeboat reappeared, the sailors struggling to pull alongside while the passengers ran from port to starboard hoping for a better view. Eliza stood where she was, filled with a strange, sick apprehension. No shouts of congratulation greeted the lifeboat crew. No man had been rescued from the boiling sea on this wild night.

A few warning raindrops introduced the deluge. Screaming, the girls scurried for shelter, carrying the men along with them. Alone, Eliza was quickly drenched to the skin.

She scarcely felt the hammering of the storm as she made her way up the stairway to the hurricane deck. Buffeted by each roll of the ship, she clung to every available handhold and tried to see through the downpour, but only the sound of men's voices led her to the spot where the sailors were making fast the lifeboat that they had used to no avail.

Three of the men, as wet as she, turned in astonishment when Eliza accosted them. "Who was it?" she asked.

"One of the deckhands, miss. Harry Svenson was his name."

The answer Eliza feared had come. "Harry." Her lips formed the word soundlessly as the rain streamed down her face.

Harry was gone. Harry, who had told Eliza he was a strong swimmer, had not been strong enough to win the fight with the all-conquering sea. Harry dead. Harry drowned. Brutally the thoughts took shape, pounding at Eliza's brain with ten times the force of the storm. She stood swaying in the gale and would have fallen to the deck, except that a sailor grabbed her arm. "Steady, miss."

"Hey!" another crewman called. "Look there!"

The eyes of everyone on deck turned in the direction of a pointing finger, then lifted toward the rigging. Eliza was barely able to make out, in the downpour, a dangling rope on the ladder.

"Deliberately cut," a sailor growled. "Almost in two."

No matter now. No matter whether the fall had been provoked or was accidental, the result was the same.

"You'd better go below, miss," one of the crew said. "You're soaking wet."

Eliza didn't hear him. She stood there below the rigging, not looking up, not looking anywhere. She was numb.

After a time that might have been short or might have been long, a young man of about Harry's age came up to her. "You were a friend of his, weren't you?"

Eliza nodded sorrowfully.

"I'm sorry, miss. We did the best we could."

Again Eliza nodded. She couldn't bring herself to speak.

Finally the hurricane deck emptied. The sailors hurried below to put on dry clothes, leaving Eliza alone in the storm. Darkness covered her funereally as she stood clinging to a stay. Although she was facing into the wind, she didn't turn for protection against it. Whipped and buffeted, she didn't move.

A light appeared in the wheelhouse, and from below came the tinkling of the saloon piano, hopelessly out of tune, a discordant reminder that sometime, somehow, she must go in out of the rain. But instead of working her way toward the stairs, she went to the rail and stared out over the ocean, knowing that nobody would miss her much if she too disappeared over the side.

However, even in this darkest of hours, Eliza didn't really contemplate suicide. Life had dealt her nothing but blows, and even if this one was the hardest of all to bear, somewhere she must find the strength to go on.

After a while she crept down to the empty stateroom, left her clothes in a sopping heap in the corner, and without unbraiding her dripping hair climbed up to the pipe berth, which was her one refuge from the steamer's alien world.

Sometime later Miss Drummond came in, snorted

when she found a puddle seeping across the floor, and spoke sharply to Eliza. "What's all this?"

Eliza didn't reply.

She didn't respond to Rosie either, when she stood on tiptoe close to Eliza's ear and whispered, "It was your young man, wasn't it?"

Rosie didn't press the question. She picked up Eliza's clothes, wringing them out and hanging them up to dry as best they could. She poured water out of her heavy shoes, turned them upside down, and said "Sh!" very sharply when Miss Drummond started to complain about "some people's disorderly habits."

Miss Drummond sniffed audibly, but she kept quiet and knelt on her berth rather than on the wet floor to say her prayers. Rosie, who was usually still boisterous at this time of night, went quietly to bed. Soon the only sounds were the creaking of the pipes that supported Eliza's hammock as it swung from side to side in time with the ship's roll.

Eliza lay flat on her back, thinking about Harry. He had been truly fond of her. She was sure of it now. And she wished (oh, how she wished!) that she had at least kissed him good-night.

Could it possibly have been last night that they had been so warm and happy together? All that was good and sweet and naïve about Harry swam through Eliza's mind, and she forgot that she had ever questioned his lack of ambition. She felt in the hammock's string pocket for the shell necklace and pulled it out quietly, then lay with it cradled against her face while the storm blew itself out.

Dawn came, pink and promising, while Miss Drummond snored and Rosie tossed and turned, murmuring in her sleep. The sharp edges of the shells bit into Eliza's cheek and finally she put the necklace back in its place. She was dry eyed, too dry eyed. All through the long hours now past her lids had burned painfully, but she had been unable to weep.

As soon as it was truly light, but long before the others were awake, Eliza climbed into her damp clothes and went up on deck, where she unbraided her hair and shook it out in the breeze. The sea was calm, the weather again mild. The tragedy might never have happened. Yet it had.

All day Eliza worked as if driven. She spoke to no one and nobody spoke to her. Early in the afternoon she moved the clothesline from one end of the hurricane deck to the other. She couldn't bear being close to the smokestack where Harry had so often lounged.

Before she had finished hanging up the wash Rosie appeared and eased herself down to sit on a convenient coil of rope. She looked on for a few tentative minutes, then said, "Eliza, listen to me."

Eliza still couldn't bring herself to speak, but she stopped pegging clothes to the line and bent her head.

"You'll get over this," said Rosie firmly. "I know you don't think so, but you will."

Eliza made a gesture of denial.

"It will take time." Rosie's strident voice turned soft and sympathetic. "It will take time; that's all."

Eliza met Rosie's eyes and shook her head.

Biting her lower lip, so heavily reddened that flakes of paint came off on her front teeth, Rosie edged forward. After an interval, she said, "Let me tell you a story about myself. When I wasn't much older than you, I fell hard for a boy in Brooklyn. I mean I was really crazy about him, like nothing before or since.

"Well, to tell you the truth, he was sort of out of my class, educated and all. He said his folks would die if we ever got married. I wasn't so sure." Rosie looked at Eliza speculatively. "People don't often die of disappointment nor grief.

"Anyway, after a while we started living together." Rosie pushed the curls off her forehead with a nervous hand, then sighed. "Hell, I don't suppose you even know what I'm talking about. Let me put it this way. I was in love with the guy, honest, and for a while things were great. Then his folks moved to Missouri, and he went with them, without even having the decency to say good-bye. After a bit I got a penny postcard addressed in his handwriting. It had a silly drawing and a message that read, 'Tis better to have loved and lost than never to have loved at all.' I could have killed him."

By now Eliza was alert enough to be puzzled. "Why are you telling me this?"

"Because, baby, that dumb saying is true. Can you imagine ending up like poor Miss Drummond, afraid to let herself go because she might get hurt or she might get cheated? Good Lord, I've been cheated by a dozen men, but do you see me whining? Not Rosie Brennan!"

"You're a very strong person, Rosie."

"Me? I'm a pushover, dearie. You're stronger than I am by far." She tugged at her stays, which were pinching. "And you're going to make a good life for yourself. You mark my words!"

As Rosie got up and started to walk away, Eliza called after her, "Your boy didn't die!"

Turning, Rosie called back with a wry grin, "Better if he had, maybe. It wouldn't have hurt so bad." Then she went on toward the circular staircase that led to the deck below.

That night Eliza slept. Her grief was still too great for tears, but she was so worn out that she slept dreamlessly. In the morning she got up and went about her work as usual, no longer locked in silence. She was very quiet, but then she had always been quiet, so nobody noticed. And nobody, except Rosie and possibly Miss Drummond, knew that she was being brave.

As if in reaction to Eliza's sorrow, and possibly to prove a point, Rosie became more obstreperous than ever. She teased every susceptible man on the ship, made fun of Mr. Mercer openly, and aroused Miss Drummond's shocked disapproval. When she walked into the stateroom one afternoon and found Rosie applying henna to her fading hair with an old toothbrush, she was utterly horrified. Rushing from the cabin, she came on Eliza in the hall and gasped, "As if paint and powder aren't quite enough to put off any decent-living soul. But on top of that she dyes her hair! Imagine!"

Not only Rosie Brennan's behavior, but that of some of the other young ladies in his charge, led Mr. Mercer to take action. He arrived in the saloon one morning after breakfast bearing large cartons in either hand. While the girls gathered around curiously, he unpacked them, distributing big skeins of yarn and suggesting that instead of getting into mischief the young ladies could keep themselves busy knitting socks.

Some agreed pleasantly enough, seizing the wool and hurrying off to find men who could be persuaded to hold the skeins while they wound the yarn into balls.

"Who are the socks to be for?" Eliza heard Mr. Conant ask, as he was pressed into service by little Miss Stevens.

"We don't really know," she answered lightly, "but Mr. Mercer promises that we'll hold a fair when we get to Seattle and sell them to help pay for all his expense and trouble on our behalf."

Sally Marshall managed to stifle an unbecoming snort. She and others who had paid their full fare were not so agreeable, and when on another day Mr. Mercer brought out some cloth with which to make men's shirts, they flatly refused to have anything to do with the project.

Some of the fabric ended up in Rosie's hands, but instead of stitching shirts on one of the sewing machines provided for the purpose, she secretly started to make a dress for Eliza. "That rag you're wearing is apt to fall in tatters around your feet," she said gruffly.

"Besides, no girl can get along with only one summer dress."

Although by nature impatient and apt to take big stitches when small ones were indicated, Rosie was surprisingly clever with a needle and quite proud of the garment she presented to Eliza.

Eliza tried on the new dress with more eagerness than she had shown about anything since Harry's death. She touched the full sleeves and the gathered waist lingeringly, so pleased that she threw her arms around Rosie's neck and hugged her. From that day on she would tolerate no criticism of Rosie from Miss Drummond or anyone else. At the slightest hint of slander she leaped to the defense of the only person, beside Harry, she had ever found truly kind.

Eliza's sixteenth birthday, on February third, happened to coincide with the date the *Continental* crossed the equator. Following an old shipboard custom, the officers and crew celebrated the occasion by holding a mock trial. Captain Windsor, dressed as King Neptune, wore a gold crown, a false white beard, and a long robe. Carrying a scepter, he held court in a sheltered section of the deck, a ceremony Eliza unfortunately missed because she was busy at her washtubs in the laundry room below.

Lunch that day was gayer than usual, with sporadic talk about "polliwogs," persons crossing the equator for the first time, and "shellbacks," the few more experienced voyagers. Eliza listened with outward equanimity, but her thoughts turned back to Harry. She wished he were here to help celebrate the day—

her birthday as well as the equator crossing—and she wished he could have seen her in the new dress, which she was planning to wear when some special occasion presented itself.

For day after day the weather stayed glorious. The sun shone, the sea was flat, and the ship picked up speed, regaining the time lost on the night of the storm. Hours of light and darkness were equally divided on the equator, and after supper almost everyone went on deck to see the Southern Cross, a constellation outlined by four great stars that had served as a guide to navigators for hundreds of years.

Eliza found herself at the rail near Alexander Stenn, who had managed to see that Miss Turner was by his side. The sky was so filled with stars that Thankful had trouble picking out the Cross among them, and Mr. Stenn seemed quite delighted when she turned to him for help.

"Look for the brightest star of all," he suggested.

Thankful pointed a dainty finger. "There?"

"That's it, the farthest to the south. It's a star of the first magnitude. Now try to find the eastern and northern stars. They aren't quite as bright, because they're of the second magnitude. Got them?"

"I think so," Thankful replied uncertainly.

"Don't look for the exact form of a cross," Mr. Stenn advised. "Actually, it's a little lopsided."

Thankful stifled a yawn and started glancing around to find some other nearby man who might be more entertaining. Mr. Stenn found that he was talking to himself when he went on to explain that the western star was of the third magnitude. Restless and bored, Thankful had moved away.

Eliza, on the other hand, had been listening with interest. "Please, what is magnitude?" she asked.

"Greatness or size, ordinarily," replied Mr. Stenn, although his voice lost its enthusiasm. "In astronomy, however, it also means brightness, because that's the way scientists measure the fixed stars with telescopes."

So many words were unfamiliar. Eliza supposed that astronomy meant the study of stars, but she had no idea how a telescope worked. Because the opportunity was at hand and too good to miss, she kept asking questions, and although his glance kept wandering in search of Thankful, he was astonishingly clear in his answers. "You're a good teacher," Eliza said.

Mr. Stenn chuckled in amusement. "I should hope so."

"Will you teach in Seattle?" Eliza asked.

Nodding, he said with pride, "I've been promised a post in Mr. Mercer's university."

"How splendid," breathed Eliza respectfully, which seemed to please Mr. Stenn inordinately, perhaps because among the male passengers aboard he did not shine like even a minor star. Girls like Thankful never sought him out. They found him tedious.

At that moment Mrs. Windsor came hurrying to Eliza. "Please get a couple of pans of boiling water from the galley and bring it to the Welds' cabin," she told her quickly. "Mrs. Weld has gone into labor. She is about to have her baby."

"Where's the doctor?" asked Roger Conant, who

was passing by with a young lady on his arm. He was referring to an elderly dentist who was the only medically trained person aboard.

The captain's wife, usually pleasant and polite to everyone, appeared to be at the end of her patience. "Dr. Barnard got into a bottle of brandy this afternoon," she told the reporter briskly. "At the moment he's three sheets to the wind, staggering around his stateroom and singing at the top of his lungs. He'll be no help at all!"

What help she could be herself Eliza hadn't the faintest idea. She knew nothing about the process of giving birth, nor did she particularly want to, and only hoped that her services would not be required once the pots of hot water were delivered.

Chapter 7

Not until four o'clock in the morning, however, did Eliza totter back to her stateroom, dead for sleep. Mrs. Windsor had been remarkably cool and efficient, as befitted a captain's wife accustomed to the emergencies of shipboard living, but she hadn't released her young assistant until a baby daughter, delivered after hours of struggle, was resting comfortably in her mother's arms.

Eliza slept until noon, barely stirring when her roommates got up. As she awakened slowly, thoughts and impressions floated to the surface of her mind in a confusing medley. The astonishment in Harry's eyes when he had discovered her hidden in the lifeboat. The radiance in Mrs. Weld's expression when she reached up to receive her newborn child. Rosie talking about love and strength and about a boy from Brooklyn who had deserted her. Men and women together. Amelia Endicott's urge to marry. Solemn Miss Drummond, wrapped in virtue. Courage to face pain. The agony of childbirth, seen at firsthand. Fragments of experience, all part of living, of learning to deal with life. And finally, an infant's first mewing cry, which quickly changed to a lusty wail.

When Eliza finally dressed and went to lunch, the happy father, a young shoemaker, had already appeared in the saloon with the tiny creature in his arms. "Isn't she beautiful?" he asked.

Remarkable, in that she made such a difficult entrance into the world, thought Eliza, but beautiful, no. She was astonished at the coos and cries of the women who clustered around Mr. Weld, pronouncing the child adorable, when Eliza could see she was far from pretty, with a red face, a kitten's unseeing eyes, and a round head brushed faintly with straight dark hair.

"Have you named her yet?" asked Sally Marshall, when she could get close enough for a good look.

The shoemaker smiled. "We're thinking of calling her Continentalla. Because she was born on board this ship."

Continentalla was a thriving baby who cried very little. By the time the lighthouse at Cape Frio was sighted a week later off the coast of Brazil, Mrs. Weld also ventured on deck. The little family sought out a sheltered corner away from the other passengers, where they sat for hours wrapped in private bliss, quite unconscious of the beauties of Rio de Janeiro's harbor. They saw nothing, spoke of nothing but their infant daughter.

Rosie was wildly excited by the prospect of going

ashore. She was tired of the long days of seeing only an unbroken seascape. Dressed in her spiffiest clothes, powdered and rouged, she looked eagerly at the mountains reaching down to finger a golden beach and sighed with impatience as the ship approached anchorage.

Seen from afar, the town of Rio did not look impressive to Eliza. She could scarcely believe Mr. Mercer's claim that it had four hundred thousand inhabitants. From the harbor it looked more like a straggling seashore village backed by green cliffs and built upon glittering sand. On some of the hills were mud houses painted in gay colors, and on others were big homes that looked like pictures of Spanish castles Eliza had once seen in a schoolbook. From this distance they looked improbably romantic. A dream.

To Rosie's exasperation, Mr. Mercer issued an order that no one could leave the *Continental* until he and the captain went ashore and investigated the situation. All day she stormed up and down the deck, protesting such treatment, and was mollified only slightly when one of the officers counseled patience. "We're apt to be laying over well on to a week," he said.

Eliza was satisfied, that first day, simply to gaze out at the harbor scene. Two other United States steamers, the *Shamokin* and the *Onward*, lay at anchor, along with several merchantmen, and among the ships plied small boats filled either with dark-skinned Brazilians or with American officers in their best uniforms.

Whenever a boat passed close to the *Continental*, its occupants craned their necks to get a closer look at the dozens of young ladies crowding close to the rail. Many of the girls waved handkerchiefs in greeting, some as impatient as Rosie to get ashore.

The day dragged on, darkness fell, and still Mr. Mercer didn't return. Most of the passengers went to bed, but Rosie stayed up and accosted him furiously when he finally came on board. On this occasion Mr. Mercer was brisk and businesslike. "Everything will be explained tomorrow morning," he said. "I shall call you all together right after breakfast. Now good night."

The next morning Rosie again paid special attention to her appearance and put on her frilliest dress, only to hear Mr. Mercer lecture his flock on his deep responsibility for their welfare. Cholera and smallpox were present in the city, he said, and it would be unwise to allow any of the young ladies to venture ashore without his protection. In other words, if they insisted on facing the threat of disease, they must do so in his company.

Insubordination swept through the room in a wave of resentful murmurs, but only the more daring ignored the leader's behest. Rosie was among the rebels. Because she and another girl were seen making off in the launch with two of the officers, the murmurs of protest changed to demands from those left behind.

Caught in a mesh of crinolines, Mr. Mercer at last agreed to take the girls on an excursion to Rio. "But it can't be arranged until tomorrow," he said firmly, and with that concession the majority had to be content.

Nevertheless, like Rosie, some of the livelier girls managed to slip away by working on the sympathies of Roger Conant or one of the other men. Even Alexander Stenn became the center of a group of eager travelers, and before noon the launch again departed, filled with belles and their quickly recruited beaus. The girls, dressed as opulently as their wardrobes permitted, waved smugly at those left on the ship as the launch plowed toward the dock. "Good riddance," said Miss Drummond, who was left behind.

Most of the excursionists returned by sundown, but Rosie didn't show up until midnight, when she banged into the stateroom and awakened both her roommates. "Did you have a nice time?" asked Eliza with a yawn.

"Bully," replied Rosie. "Bully!" She pulled off her dress and unlaced her stays in the dark, then fell into bed in her shimmy and drawers, snoring as soon as her head touched the pillow.

"She's intoxicated," said Miss Drummond grimly to no one in particular.

On the following day the launch had to make several trips to get Mr. Mercer's troupe to the city dock. Eliza was one of those to crowd aboard the final boatload, for the first time wearing the white dress Rosie had made for her. Although she had no crinoline, the skirt was full and flattering, accentuating the smallness of her waist and the tan she had acquired from the warm southern sun.

Eliza looked forward to the excursion with pleasure, even though their arrival in Rio meant that now

Thankful could send a message about her to Salem. Still, a month or more would elapse before it could arrive, so she had nothing to fear at the moment.

Nevertheless, Eliza intentionally tagged along at the rear of the procession led by Mr. Mercer down the principal street. She didn't want to attract his attention in any way, for fear he would recognize the shirting cloth of which her dress was made. Furthermore, she hadn't dared ask permission to join the party. She had simply slipped into the launch at the last minute, a wren among chattering birds of a brighter feather, but equally eager to fly away from the nest.

Along the line of march dozens of men stood back to let the girls pass. Most were black slaves, wearing nothing but pantaloons strapped to their gleaming torsos with leather belts. They nudged each other and chuckled at the sight of the ladies, abroad in the daytime without the protection of a carriage.

Toward the center of the city the streets grew so narrow that small hacks drawn by one mule occupied nearly the entire width, forcing the girls back along the walls until Mr. Mercer could hurry them toward a large square. There a handsome coach emblazoned with the royal coat of arms passed so close to the party that Eliza caught a glimpse of the emperor and his family inside. The girls became so excited that they began waving their handkerchiefs madly, a breach of etiquette for which they were scolded by Mr. Mercer. "You will please not act like a bunch of silly schoolgirls!" he berated his charges. Even Eliza felt daunted.

After pointing out the palace, a low stuccoed building that to the New Englanders looked more like a factory boardinghouse than an emperor's residence, Mr. Mercer led his unwieldy group to another square, covered with green grass and dominated by a huge central fountain spilling water into an encircling basin. Dozens of women were washing clothes, but others lounged idly on the grass, talking and laughing as if they didn't have a care in the world.

"These are the poor of the city," Mr. Mercer said, his face assuming a prim expression. "You can see that most of them are loafers, here as well as everywhere else."

Eliza saw something quite different, people who looked merry and well fed and friendly. They didn't stare at the girls from the *Continental* suspiciously, but seemed lazily pleased with the visit of the foreigners.

Peddlers went by—a broom man, a lace seller, a couple of peanut vendors—singing praises of their wares in lilting Portuguese. A young woman with skin the color of coffee with cream sat on the grass unashamedly nursing a baby, while a trio of girls from the Mercer expedition whispered behind their hands in maidenly distaste. Several dark-skinned women were smoking long-stemmed pipes, which shocked Mr. Mercer and moved him to round up his flock, some of whom had taken to running here and there like scatter-brained chickens.

Before long it became evident that the large group was uncontrollable, so the girls were arbitrarily divided into parties, one under the guidance of Mr.

Conant, who proposed taking his group to the market, while Mr. Mercer intended to proceed with the other to the botanical gardens.

While negotiations between the two men were under way, Eliza wandered across the grass toward a group of people surrounding a frolicsome mulatto dancer. She wore three full skirts, red, yellow, and black, and her head was bound in a turban draped with such style that Eliza was captivated. Singing her own accompaniment in a high, clear voice, the woman swung and swooped like some rare tropical bird, joyous and unself-conscious.

The scene was so wonderfully strange and colorful that Eliza stood fascinated until the dancer broke off as her audience turned toward a commotion at the fountain. A handsome Brazilian with a finger to his lips and a twinkle in his eye had crept up behind a pretty girl who was up to her elbows in foaming water. Suddenly seizing her by the feet, he tipped her head-first into the suds, eliciting a shout of laughter from the bystanders. The girl struggled to her feet, kicked a spray of water in her tormentor's direction, and climbed over the side of the basin to chase him across the square, laughing as hard as any of the rest.

Barefoot and brown, dressed in a sheer blouse and clinging skirt, the washerwoman obviously wore no underclothes at all, but she seemed not in the least embarrassed and sauntered back to the fountain unhurriedly, wringing out her wet skirt on the way.

There was something carefree and natural about the life here in Brazil that made Eliza feel she had come from another planet. Until she glanced around the square a few minutes later she was quite unaware that the group from the ship had moved on.

This discovery didn't trouble her especially, although she was eager to see the market. The hills rose sharply at her back, and the ocean waves rolled gently to a beach she could glimpse by looking ahead. It was impossible to get lost in Rio. She could easily find her way back to the dock.

Meanwhile, the market attracted her more than the beach, but she had no idea of its direction. She approached the nursing mother. "Market?" she asked, spreading her hands and looking around.

Nonplused by the English word, the woman looked up and shook her head. Her black eyes were soft and questioning, but she couldn't be helpful. *"Nao compreender,"* she apologized.

Eliza's inquiry did not go unnoticed. Several people strolled over, and she repeated her question, hoping that someone would understand. As it happened, the young man who had dunked the girl in the basin came up just then and asked a question in Portuguese.

"Market," Eliza repeated without much hope.

"Aha!" he cried. *"Mercado!"* Grinning, he pointed toward a street that led back toward the hills. *"Ao mercado!"* Then he said slowly in English, "I go. Show you way."

Eliza wasn't sure that she wanted such a prankster as a guide, although she wasn't especially uneasy when he insisted upon accompanying her. To the delight of the crowd, he swept off an imaginary hat, made a low bow, then said, "Doña, follow me, please."

Eliza followed. Sometimes in single file, sometimes abreast, they hurried through the narrow streets. "You speak quite a few words of English," Eliza told her escort after a while.

The fellow flashed a wide smile, white teeth gleaming against his flawless brown skin. "I work for *ingles* —English man," he explained carefully. "He teach me, yes?"

"Yes," said Eliza.

"You teach me too? I like that."

Eliza looked doubtful.

"How you say *mercado?*"

"Market."

"Market," repeated the young man happily. Then he advanced their acquaintanceship a step further by saying, "My name Paulo."

"Hello, Paulo." Eliza ventured a friendly smile.

Delighted, Paulo pointed a finger in the general direction of Eliza's chest. "You?"

"My name is Eliza."

"Ah, Doña Eliza. Very nice."

Edging around a man carrying a heavy tray of bananas on his head, Eliza found herself within sight of the native street market. Shoppers were weaving past baskets of produce spread on the ground, waiting in line at rickety stalls, and exchanging Brazilian *cruzeiros* for all sorts of meat, vegetables, giant flowers, and unfamiliar fruits.

Some of the latter Paulo pointed to and named. "*Sapoti*," he said, indicating a fruit the size and shape of a small black-skinned peach. He gave the market woman a copper and selected two from the pile, one for Eliza and one for himself.

"Good," he said, as he bit through the soft skin.

Eliza found the inside of the *sapoti* white and sweet, tasting faintly like licorice. "Very good," she agreed. This approval led Paulo to insist that she try another fruit, called a *pinia*, which looked like a pinecone and came apart in segments. Piles of mangoes and papayas, however, he passed by. "Easy to pick from trees," he said.

Near the meat section of the *mercado* there were monkeys and parrots for sale, a sight that offended Eliza's New England upbringing, because flies buzzed indiscriminately around the cages and the butchers' stalls. In the nearby street barefoot men trotted along carrying baskets either balanced on their heads or slung on long poles across their shoulders. They maintained a bouncing, rhythmic pace as they avoided a multitude of heavily laden burros, which were being switched indolently by their owners from the rear.

"You like market, Doña Eliza?" asked Paulo with a grin.

Although the stench of the meat and fish was beginning to nauseate her, Eliza tried to be polite. "Very interesting," she praised, "but I must go now. You see, my friends have already left, and I mustn't be late."

"You go where?"

"Back to the ship. The *Continental*."

"Aha, you go by beach. I walk with you."

"Thank you, but I can find my way alone."

Paulo shook his head. "I walk."

And walk with Eliza he did, taking her down a quieter street to the sunlit beach, where he tried to persuade her to take off her shoes and go barefoot, which he obviously considered the only sensible way to walk on sand. When she refused, he did the next best thing and took her down to the edge of the tideline, where the sand was firmer, then started off with her toward the distant port.

There were a number of other people on the beach, boys and girls walking hand in hand, a young couple stopping impetuously to kiss, a very old woman in a long black dress wading waist high into the ocean to take a bath. A few young boys were swimming, others were building sand castles, and one or two were sailing paper kites that looked like bright-colored birds. There were no little girls anywhere in sight.

Eliza trudged along in her sensible boots, which were out of keeping with her white summer dress but the only footgear she owned. A sweetmeat peddler passed, crying his wares in a little song that made Eliza smile.

"You want?" Paulo asked quickly.

"No. But I love the music."

"Music?" Paulo's brow wrinkled.

"Song, like this." Eliza trilled a few bars in imitation.

Paulo grinned. "Aha, music." He whistled a dance tune and pretended to strum a guitar.

Around Guadabara Bay the beach curved in a giant arc, like a new moon tossed casually at the edge of the water. There were islands offshore, and on a short peninsula an oddly shaped mountain fingered the sky. Paulo stopped clowning and pointed to it proudly. "The Corcovado," he said. "Very fine!"

The February sun was hot, and Eliza's feet were beginning to hurt. (Actually, she had outgrown the boots months before.) Noticing that she was limping, Paulo called to a beach vendor who had festoons of native clogs slung over his shoulders. "You need *tamancos*," he told Eliza. "Here, you buy."

Eliza had nothing but North American money in her possession, but when she gave the fellow a half dollar, he took the coin, bit it to make sure it was silver, and gave her two *cruzeiros* in change. Once her boots were off, Eliza felt a lot better, and padded along in the clogs quite comfortably.

Paulo looked pleased. "You like?"

"Very much."

"Good." Paulo insisted on carrying Eliza's heavy boots, which he examined curiously and with considerable distaste.

"For winter," she tried to explain, and then realized that the word winter would be beyond Paulo's understanding. Rio was a place of perpetual summer. How could he imagine snow or the cold of February in Salem? She spread her hands, laughed, and gave up.

When they came within sight of the port, Paulo seemed regretful that their time together was growing short. Slowly they approached the dock where the launch was tied up, and Paulo said good-bye, but not before taking Eliza's hand and squeezing it warmly.

Mr. Mercer, counting off the number of young ladies he was handing aboard, happened to glance toward the beach and saw this parting gesture. With an audible gasp he staggered backward, his face muscles stiffening. As soon as she came within reach, he grasped Eliza's arm roughly. "What under the sun have you been *doing?*" he hissed.

Chapter 8

"Leave the door open!" Mr. Mercer barked.

Eliza, who had been summoned to his stateroom as soon as everyone in the botanical-gardens group was back on board or accounted for, did as she was told and stood waiting for the inevitable scolding. In order not to add fuel to the newly lit fire, she had changed back to her usual dress. There was no need to flaunt the white shirting material in Mr. Mercer's face.

"I am ashamed of you, Eliza. Deeply ashamed!" he said.

Eliza stood with her hands clasped behind her back. She supposed she would be accused of stealing the cotton cloth for the new dress.

"You realize, I hope, that the young ladies who have placed themselves in my charge for this voyage are from highly respectable backgrounds."

With a few exceptions, Eliza thought, but the meekness of her demeanor did not change.

"I find your behavior deeply shocking," Mr. Mercer said, emphasizing the adjective.

Eliza looked up and met his eyes inquiringly.

"Consorting with a Negro, in broad daylight, on the beach!" Mr. Mercer rested a hand, as if for support, on a chair back. His voice rose to an agonized screech. "Holding hands!"

So that was it! Not the white dress, after all. Eliza, relieved, said, "Paulo only took my hand for a moment, to say good-bye."

"Paulo. You even know his name? What sort of example are you setting for the rest of my female passengers. You, a common stowaway, who should try to be self-effacing and thank your Maker that I've permitted you to return to this ship!"

The thought that Mr. Mercer could put her ashore permanently in Brazil had never crossed Eliza's mind. Admittedly, she still needed his protection, but she couldn't understand why her encounter with Paulo had provoked such wrath.

"Where did you find this—this darkie? How did you meet him?"

Remembering the circumstances, a ghost of a smile touched Eliza's lips, but when she tried to explain, Mr. Mercer's rage only increased.

"So you picked him up in the square, like a common tramp."

"Paulo isn't a tramp," said Eliza artlessly. "He works for—"

"My God!" Mr. Mercer broke in. "Don't you understand anything?" He was bellowing now, his freckled face red with indignation. "While we are in this port you will remain on shipboard, Eliza. You are in disgrace!"

Several passengers had gathered outside the stateroom door to listen to this tirade, and by sundown half the ship had heard the story. "It's a wonder he didn't have the captain clap you in the brig," said Rosie with a laugh. "Like they did the first mate."

This development was news to Eliza. "Mr. Corrigan? Why?"

Unaccountably embarrassed, Rosie tried to change the subject, but Eliza persisted. "Tell me why."

"There was no need you should know," said Rosie gently, "but he's said to have had a grudge against your Harry, and he managed to see that one of the ropes in the rigging ladder was cut."

"Then sent Harry aloft?" Eliza whispered, sick at heart that the suspicions on the night of the storm should be confirmed.

"That's about it."

In comparison, Eliza's transgression was minor indeed. Gradually she was able to sort things out and keep her perspective, accepting Mr. Mercer's decree that she could go on no further excursions and watching the other girls disembark without particular envy. She had had her day in the sun.

While she washed and ironed and hung clothes up to dry in the offshore breeze Eliza's thoughts once more returned to Harry. Feature by feature she rebuilt his image—blue eyes, blond hair, clean-shaven, clear complexion—but his immediacy was diminishing. At last Eliza was able to recognize that Rosie's prediction had been right. Time was on her side. The healing process had begun.

Little by little, as her horizons broadened, Eliza was growing in experience as well as in years. On this voyage she had already encountered not only death but birth, and she had heard the first feeble cries of a new-born infant. She had met a stranger from a strange and beautiful land who was companionable and fun to be with, whatever the color of his skin. She had also found a good friend—no matter how unlikely—in Rosie Brennan.

Concerning Mr. Mercer, Eliza was still ambivalent. His good qualities, imagination and zest, did not escape her, yet his narrow-mindedness and suspiciousness seemed pitiable.

Few of the other girls pitied the "old man," however. They teased and taunted him, accepted his dictums unwillingly, and laughed behind their hands at his ill-fated attempts at courtship. He had been wooing several young ladies in turn to no avail, even while he made strict rules concerning the behavior of the rest.

When, after nearly a week, the *Continental* steamed out of the harbor of Rio, heading away from Brazil toward the Straits of Magellan, Mr. Mercer launched a new crusade. Faced anew by the boredom of long days at sea, groups of men and girls began to while away the hours by playing Copenhagen or whist. The games were innocent enough, but Mr. Mercer was opposed to card playing on principle, and he was especially annoyed to discover that some of the officers were participating in the fun.

On Sundays he took to sermonizing about vice in all its aspects, and one evening he stormed into the saloon and dispersed a table of whist players, driving them up on deck. By now, however, his charges were openly defiant. When Mr. Mercer established a ten o'clock curfew, they ignored it. When he reiterated his command that his young ladies were not to associate with the ship's officers, they paraded their conquests before his eyes.

The late February days dragged slowly on. Miss Stevens, in her lifeboat classroom, used up her limited store of general information, along with her knowledge of arithmetic, which stopped at fractions. One morning Eliza came upon the teacher beseeching Alexander Stenn to help out and give a lesson in the geography of South America, which she found herself unable to do without the aid of a proper text.

"Oh, Mr. Stenn, please! They won't sit still. They fidget and fuss. It's all quite beyond me." Tears filled the unhappy lady's eyes. "Sometimes I wish I hadn't started the whole thing."

"Now, now," said Mr. Stenn comfortingly. "It's better than having the children scampering about the decks. I'll see what I can do."

Since there was a fine drizzle—no morning to hang out washing!—Eliza followed along to the lifeboat, where Miss Stevens introduced her new assistant with all the ceremony she would have accorded a visiting professor from Harvard. "Now, children," she said, "you can ask Mr. Stenn all the questions you usually put to me."

There was utter silence.

Alexander Stenn lowered himself to a wooden seat and cleared his throat. "Do any of you know where we are right now?" he asked.

"In a lifeboat," replied one of the older boys impudently.

Mr. Stenn laughed, peering at the lad through his thick-lensed glasses. "What latitude, what longitude?"

"Who cares?"

"You'd care if you were captain of this ship, or captain of any other ship, for that matter," Mr. Stenn shot back. "Have you ever heard of Magellan?"

The boy slumped sulkily against an oarlock. Nobody else volunteered a reply.

Alexander Stenn cleared his throat and leaned forward, resting his elbows on his bony knees, and said conversationally, "In a few days the *Continental* is going to enter the Straits, named for a very remarkable man. Not long after Columbus discovered America, a good-looking Portuguese named Ferdinand Magellan set out from Spain with a fleet of five sailing ships. He landed in the bay at Rio, just as we did, but can you imagine how wild Brazil was more than three hundred years ago?" He talked along chattily, asking questions that didn't require answers, until the children stopped wriggling and began to listen to an adventure story they found no less fascinating because it was real.

Eliza listened along with the rest. She could imagine the explorer's anxiety as he cruised the coast of South America, looking for a possible passage to the western sea.

Mr. Stenn described the freezing weather into which Magellan sailed. "Can't you tell that each day now it's getting colder?" he asked the children. "You're going to have to put on winter clothes again before long, because we're likely to see some ice and snow." He told them how treacherous the passage through the Straits was bound to be and warned them all that it would be slow going for them. "But not as slow as for Magellan, because we have a steamer while he had only those sailing ships."

Unexpectedly Alexander Stenn broke off. "There's a lot more to the story," he said, "but it will have to wait until tomorrow. In the meantime, try to remember what I've said, because before I go on I'll expect each of you to answer a question about the story you've heard today."

As the children clambered out of the lifeboat and raced away Eliza followed them slowly. Catching up with her, Mr. Stenn remarked, "They're itchy little monkeys, aren't they? Do you think they learned anything at all?"

"I think so," replied Eliza carefully. She turned and smiled. "Anyway, you'll know tomorrow, won't you?"

Alexander Stenn took off his glasses and polished

them on his pocket handkerchief. "I expect so," he said. Then he added, "Although I yearn for the day when I'll teach university students, it's rather interesting to talk to children and try to stimulate their minds. Not that I'd consider grammar-school teaching as a career, mind you. My work will be at the university level in Seattle."

He might have continued had he not spotted Thankful and Sally at the starboard rail watching a school of flying fish. In the distance a green coastline seemed to flow along beside the ship, and once in a while the girls looked up and regarded it ruefully. There were no houses, no villages, only tree-covered hills and occasional mountains. Now that Rio was far behind, ennui was inevitable. So much so that the girls called to Mr. Stenn, "Come over here, professor! You can help us settle a dispute."

Whenever Thankful beckoned, Mr. Stenn went eagerly. Without taking time to excuse himself, he left Eliza, who walked on a few paces, then stopped to watch some dolphins bounding in the wake of the flying fish.

"It's like this," she heard Sally say in a trilling voice. "Thankful has a friend who ordered a pair of stays. You *do* know what stays are, professor?"

Alexander Stenn nodded, flushing as he always did when he was being teased.

"They were made of very stiff whalebone," Thankful broke in, "and they measured fourteen inches around the waist. My friend's waist was eighteen inches, but she had the laces tightened an inch a day until she finally got the edges of the stays to meet. Can you imagine?"

Mr. Stenn shook his head. "It must have been terribly painful."

"Oh, it was simply killing," Thankful replied, "but my friend dearly loved to look fashionable."

"What is the dispute then?"

Sally answered, "I claim it must have been unhealthy, as well as painful. What do you think, Mr. Stenn? Tell us the truth."

Eliza could see that he was faced with a dilemma. He wanted to please Thankful but was too honest to take her side. Instead, he tried to dodge the issue. "Fashion has always been perverse," he said in a rather didactic manner. "Chinese women still bind their feet, and the French are responsible for the style of tight lacing. I wonder which is worse?"

Thankful stamped her foot. "You are a horrid man," she told Mr. Stenn with a pretty toss of her head. "I thought you liked me."

"Oh, I do!" His reply was heartfelt.

"Then you should agree with me. If I had an eighteen-inch waist, I'd do the very same thing as my friend."

Eliza walked on, taking a turn around the deck, and when she passed the pair again, they were leaning together and giggling. Mr. Stenn had disappeared.

"He's such a tiresome man," Thankful commented, while Eliza was still within earshot. "Far too serious minded for me."

"Yet he adores you," replied Sally.

"Much good it will do him," said Thankful with a shrug. Then both girls burst out laughing.

That such a silly interchange should provoke so much mirth seemed very odd to Eliza, yet through such scraps of overheard conversations she was learning what young ladies usually talked about. None of them was particularly interested in the way the scenery was changing, becoming grand, gloomy, and peculiarly un-inviting as the steamer moved steadily toward the Straits. There were no more big harbors like Rio along the way, but the *Continental* stopped at a couple of small, nondescript ports.

Meanwhile, the girls languished. They craved enter-tainment, and there was little to be had. The more diligent knitters had finished their socks, and the seam-stresses had piled several shirts, indifferently tailored, on a table in the saloon. A few followed Eliza's prac-tice of taking books from the library, but rarely were the volumes actually read.

Roger Conant alone seemed fully occupied. At al-most any time of day he could be found with a pad of paper on his knees, writing away busily. Rosie came by and looked over his shoulder one morning, reading his closely written, slanting script. "Why, Rod," she cried after a few minutes, "all you're doing is describ-ing the scenery. Nobody in New York will care a rap about that. They'll want to read about us girls!"

Overhearing, Eliza felt sure that Rosie was right. Newspaper readers would certainly be more interested in Mr. Conant's "virgins" than they would be in the mountains of Chile or Brazil. Maybe the private diary Mr. Conant also was keeping might prove more enlightening than the pieces he shipped back home.

" 'The scenery here is as wild and romantic as the most enthusiastic lover of nature could desire.' " Rosie pranced across the saloon mimicking Mr. Conant's voice as well as his writing style. Offended, the reporter got up to leave the room, but before he reached the door Rosie added with a chuckle, "Now I'm a lover of nature all right, but not the kind of nature Rod means."

Even Rosie was impressed, however, when at noon that same day the *Continental* passed through Glacier Bay. On its rocky shoreline was a deep gorge filled with ice and snow, so overshadowed by cliffs that the sun never reached it. Even on this comparatively mild March day the water running down the rock sides froze as it hit the glacier.

Alexander Stenn, surrounded by children, was explaining the manner in which glaciers are formed, while Miss Stevens stood nearby, nodding her head from time to time in approval. Eliza noticed that the children seemed interested. Apparently the professor's lessons were proving a success.

By midafternoon the ship was moving slowly between high mountain walls, which were reflected starkly in the water, and the night's anchorage was bleak. "Three hundred and fifty miles of this!" Mr. Conant complained. "Aren't we getting near the end?"

"Wait until you see Port Eden!" Mr. Mercer told

his flock, trying to sound encouraging. As aware as Captain Windsor of the increasing restiveness of both passengers and crew, he was ready to promise a happier stopping place to one and all.

Indeed, by the next afternoon, the ship was sailing in tranquil waters where side-wheel ducks were basking. The air was as soft and balmy as in Salem's June, and Eliza went up on deck to watch the big birds flying on the surface of the water by using their wings rather than their feet as paddles. Behind them they left a wake like that of the side-wheel steamer that Eliza had taken from Boston to New York, but their progress didn't seem very efficient. They had a harder time getting into the air than a New England pheasant, and once up could fly only a short distance.

Nevertheless, they provided a welcome diversion, and most of the passengers stayed on deck for a long time to watch the curious birds. "You only find them in Patagonia," called Captain Windsor from the hurricane deck. "Nowhere else in the world."

In the late afternoon the ship's anchor was dropped in deep water close to a verdant shoreline, and that evening discipline was relaxed. A boatload of passengers was taken ashore, where in the chilly but lingering twilight the younger girls gathered wild flowers, while the men hauled wood for a big bonfire, around which everybody clustered to sing songs. Port Eden seemed like Eden indeed.

Eliza had been left behind, on the theory that her position on board entitled her to no special privileges.

Fair enough, she thought; the excursion to Rio had been something of a fluke. Besides, she enjoyed the party from a distance almost as much as if she had been there. The bonfire flames still leaped high, and the singers' voices were more muted and harmonious than they might have been at close range. She stood at the rail for a long time, wrapped in one of Rosie's shawls, and marveled that she was there at all.

Except for the continuing, nagging worry over money, Eliza might have considered herself happy. Lately, however, fewer people wanted their laundry done; their pocket money was dwindling. Some had spent more than they intended on trinkets in Rio. Others had bought wine or spirits. Several of the more prosperous passengers who had welcomed Eliza's services at the beginning of the trip now began to conserve their United States dollars by doing their own wash.

When Eliza took her week's earnings to Mr. Mercer the next morning, she could hand over only eighty-five cents. He looked at the coins with annoyance. "What's this?"

"That's all I earned this week," Eliza told him. "I'm sorry, but I'm afraid a good many people are getting short of cash."

"This won't do! It won't do at all."

Eliza could only repeat, "I'm sorry." She considered promising to pay him part of her earnings when she found work in Seattle, but she wanted to cancel her debt to Mrs. Endicott first. While she stood looking unhappily at the coins flung on the stateroom table, Mr. Mercer begged Heaven to deliver him from his tribulations, especially from this unobliging, ignorant servant girl.

Escaping at last, Eliza felt as properly chastised as though she had been struck with a stick. She did her best to forget the words shouted after her. "I've a good mind to put you off at Lota! I can, you know!"

Chapter 9

Lota!

"Where is Lota?" Eliza asked Rosie late that night. She trusted it wasn't in Patagonia, such a wild and forbidding land.

"Lota? Search me." Rosie, who was half asleep, drew the blanket, too thin for this climate, around her shoulders. "Why should you care?"

"Mr. Mercer threatens to put me off the ship there. He's annoyed because I'm not earning enough money anymore."

"Lota is in Chile," said Miss Drummond from her berth. She joined in conversation only occasionally and never wasted words.

"I think the old man's talking through his hat," Rosie offered with a yawn. "I doubt he can put anybody off this ship without Captain Windsor's say-so." After a pause for consideration, she added, "Forget it, Eliza. He's bound to be bluffing."

"I think so too," Eliza agreed, "but you can't be

sure. Remember those poor people he put off at Sandy Hook?"

"While he hid in the coal bin." Rosie chuckled. "He won't try that stunt twice. But if you're worried, go to the captain. Throw yourself on his mercy. Spill a few tears. He's a decent sort, even if he does treat his officers like naughty schoolboys when they stray out-of-bounds."

Instead of approaching the captain, Eliza went to Mrs. Windsor the next morning and explained her concern. "Do you think Mr. Mercer could do such a thing?" she asked.

"I consider it most unlikely," Mrs. Windsor said comfortingly. "In any case, I'll speak to my husband. Somebody should keep an eye on you."

Ever since the night of Continentalla's birth Mrs. Windsor had treated Eliza with special consideration. This morning was no exception. She turned away to attend to a question from the cook, but not before she patted Eliza's shoulder and said firmly, "Stop worrying, child."

Eliza tried, unsuccessfully, to follow Mrs. Windsor's advice. Money, which Mr. Mercer described in his Sunday sermons as the root of all evil, to her seemed to be the root of all security and happiness. She wondered if people with money were ever threatened, ever frightened? It appeared extremely doubtful. People with money were able to do as they chose.

Although her pride suffered, Eliza went to her more faithful customers and begged for work. Some were sympathetic but few were helpful. Rio had drained the purses of many of the men, who had taken to washing their own shirts. A few employed Eliza to iron them, but pickings were slim.

Rosie remained loyal, but her resources had dwindled also, and the dollar a week she had offered Eliza at the outset of the voyage had been reduced to fifty cents. Miss Drummond never had been known to spend a nickel, and most of the thrifty New Englanders were loathe to part with their remaining cash. Eliza found herself all but unemployed.

Recalling the proverb "out. of sight, out of mind," she spent a good part of each day trying to keep out of Mr. Mercer's way. For hours at a time she lay in her pipe berth, reading. Miss Stevens had recently introduced her to Dickens, and *David Copperfield* occupied her for long days. She suffered with him, identified with him, and felt that his life was more real and far more tragic than her own. Mr. Mercer's personality paled when compared to David's stepfather, Mr. Murdstone. Now there was a man really to hate and fear!

When Eliza did venture out on deck, she found a secluded spot from which she could watch the changing scenery. After a complicated passage through rock-bound basins, the ship at last emerged into the Gulf of Penas and the calm waters of the aptly named Pacific Ocean. A few days later, on a cloudless Sunday morning, Eliza was awakened by Rosie's shout that they must go up on deck at once. On the horizon several vessels could be seen under full sail.

Most of the girls, even those who habitually slept late, were already up on the hurricane deck. The gloom of the past fortnight, broken only by the brief stop at Port Eden, had at last lifted. Everyone seemed cheerful and full of anticipation. Lota apparently lay ahead.

Only Eliza found the name of the port sinister. She was not due to take her week's pay to Mr. Mercer until the next morning, but since she had again earned under a dollar she intended to delay as long as possible. She trusted Mrs. Windsor as much as she dared, but she distrusted Mr. Mercer even more.

In the meantime, the morning was indeed glorious, the sailing ships a joy to watch. One of them, a frigate with all canvas set, was headed in the same direction as the *Continental* and excited the special interest of the passengers, who crowded to the port rail.

"Can you see if she's flying a United States flag?" Thankful, who was short-sighted but would have perished at the thought of wearing spectacles, put the question to Eliza, who happened to be standing next to her.

"Not yet," replied Eliza, shading her eyes with one hand.

"Who has the binoculars?" a male voice called.

Nobody seemed to know.

"Oh, I do hope there are plenty of young officers on board!" Sally Marshall was quivering with excitement.

"American officers," Thankful suggested hopefully.

"They can be Hottentots for all I care," called Rosie gaily, "as long as they have warm hearts and deep pockets."

"Rosie Brennan, you're a caution!"

"I only say what the rest of you think!"

The badinage continued as the two ships moved onward, still far apart but following the same general course. Alexander Stenn, having found the binoculars, squeezed in next to Thankful. "It's a man-of-war," he decided after taking a long look, and almost at once the officers within earshot agreed with him.

"A warship?" squealed Thankful. "Who's at war?"

"Chile and Spain," explained one of the engineers. "They've been fighting for almost a full year. The Chileans won their independence from Spain back in 1810, but now they're at it again. The Spanish fleet has captured several key Chilean ports and blockaded them. I wonder what the outcome will be this time?"

"Has the United States become involved?" inquired Dr. Barnard, who was relatively sober this morning.

"Not yet, but I hear there's talk of it."

"Then that ship can't be one of ours," said Dr. Barnard in disappointment. A moment later he asked, "What are those puffs of smoke?"

"Looks like a signal gun," Alexander Stenn muttered.

"Aimed at us? Can she want us to stop?" asked Roger Conant from some distance away.

"Poof," said an officer. "Lota is a free port, not under the Spanish blockade. We checked it carefully." He squinted at the distant ship and said, "I'll wager the captain makes a run for it. He dearly loves a race."

"Full speed ahead," came the order from the bridge at the same moment, and the passengers cheered as the *Continental* surged forward, plowing through the water with less grace than the frigate, but with enough power to bring her quickly abreast.

The ship could now be seen to be flying a Spanish flag, but neither the officers nor Captain Windsor seemed concerned. Still running under full steam, the *Continental* swept ahead into the entrance of a harbor protected by a headland stretching like a finger into the sea.

"Hurray!" yelled Rosie, bluff and gusty with delight. "We won!"

"That'll send the Spaniard off with a flea in his ear," predicted Dr. Barnard. His gray hair was tossed by the breeze, and his usually bleary eyes were bright.

Alexander Stenn wasn't so sure. "Look," he said to Thankful, and pointed back to the narrow entrance. "She's dropping sail."

"Maybe she'll follow us in," suggested Thankful.

"Spanish officers would be better than nothing," Rosie whooped.

"*Defeated* Spanish officers?" questioned Sally, but Rosie didn't answer, because at that moment it became apparent that Captain Windsor's headlong arrival had created a commotion on shore. Half a hundred people were crowding to the dock, some running downhill on foot while others, on horseback, were skidding at a breakneck pace down steep paths that crisscrossed the bluffs.

"What do you suppose is happening?" asked little Miss Stevens.

"We're really creating a sensation," breathed Thankful happily.

"Maybe they want to see what Yankee girls are made of," suggested Rosie with another roar of laughter. She sounded ready for any sort of reception that might be in store.

While the crowd at the water's edge thickened, the *Continental*'s crew lowered the anchor, and as soon as a boat could be launched Captain Windsor was rowed ashore. He seemed to Eliza to be in a great hurry. Shortly, in an even greater hurry, he returned.

Rumors began to race among the passengers. Was there an epidemic in Lota? Smallpox? Typhoid? Were the Chilean natives unfriendly? Was there no coal to be had?

A report that originally had gained no credence was finally confirmed. The captain had steamed into the wrong port! Caught up in the thrill of the race, he had rushed right by the smaller harbor of Lota and come in on the far side of the headland to the blockaded port of Coronel.

At first the passengers were amused. "That's one on the captain," crowed Dr. Barnard, slapping his knee.

"It'll take a bit to live this one down," said Roger Conant, and he wondered aloud whether the story would make good copy for the *Times*.

"It's a natural mistake," said Mr. Mercer, taking the captain's part. "Don't be too critical, Rod. You might have done the same thing."

Everyone stayed on deck, arguing the matter, while the anchor was laboriously hauled up again and the *Continental* turned to leave. Then Eliza, along with everyone else, saw a dismaying sight. The Spanish frigate was lying athwart the harbor's entrance with all portholes open. There was no way that the steamer could pass.

"Looks like they're kind of mad," suggested one of the children gathered close to Miss Stevens.

"Sh, now," counseled the teacher. "The captain knows what he's doing. We'll be all right."

She was far more sanguine than most of the other passengers. The open portholes of the man-of-war presaged a warm reception. At that very instant a cannon shot thundered from the ship and several women screamed.

"You spoke a moment too soon," Dr. Barnard said to Miss Stevens.

An officer made a trumpet of his hands and shouted, "Don't worry, folks! She's firing blanks."

Nevertheless, a number of girls bolted for the stairs, while their slower companions huddled in the shelter of the smokestack. Frozen in surprise, Eliza stayed by the rail, with Thankful and Alexander Stenn only a few paces away.

Suddenly another shot rang out. As a shell whizzed across the starboard bow Mr. Stenn pushed Thankful roughly to the deck and crouched above her protectively. "Hey, that was live!" shouted the officer less cheerfully.

Sally Marshall swooned in the willing arms of the nearest man, who happened to be Roger Conant, "Oh, Rod," she begged. "Get me away from here!"

Miss Drummond fell to her knees, hands clasped and lips moving in silent prayer. Eliza, about to go to her, was nudged by Rosie. "Wait till she sees her first Indian with a tomahawk," she whispered, far more excited than scared. A girl fleeing toward the stairs fainted in an untidy heap, her crinoline standing up like a huge hoop and her embroidered drawers clearly visible.

A flag had been raised on the intercepting ship, and although there were no further shots, the *Continental* was obliged to haul to. When it seemed safe to do so, Alexander Stenn scrambled to his feet and helped Thankful up apologetically.

Eliza, standing by, was prepared for a violent reaction on Thankful's part. But instead of being furious Thankful threw her arms around his neck and burst into tears of gratitude.

"You saved my life!" she cried hysterically. "Oh, Alex, you were wonderful. So quick! So very alert. Goodness, I could be lying here in a pool of blood." Gradually she released her grasp and stood looking up at him as though he were a new and fascinating discovery. "What can I ever do to repay you?" she asked soulfully.

"Just be kind to me."

"Oh, I will, I will. I'll never tease you again, I promise. I'll never call you professor, in fun I mean, because you're a really marvelous person and I owe you a very great debt."

Alexander looked astonished but overjoyed. He dusted Thankful's skirts with his pocket handkerchief, murmuring comforting phrases while the other brave souls who had stayed on deck watched an armed longboat leave the frigate and come alongside. Miss Drummond got to her feet in time to take a peek and immediately grasped Eliza's arm. "A villainous-looking set of cutthroats," she said in a hoarse whisper. "Come below with me! We'll barricade the stateroom door."

Eliza refused to be persuaded. The action was up on deck, and there she intended to remain. Along with the rest she watched a Spanish officer come aboard and be greeted by Captain Windsor. To the relief of everyone, the Spaniard seemed like a gentleman and behaved quite properly.

Yet the expression on his face was grim. He spoke a few curt words to Captain Windsor, then was led quickly in the direction of the officers' quarters. This development caused the girls to run around in a new flurry of consternation.

"Suppose they take us all prisoners?" Sally asked, shivering.

"And carry us to Spain?"

"Do you think we're in real danger? Oh, surely not?"

"If shooting isn't real danger, what is?"

"We could end our lives in chains, in some miserable Spanish dungeon!" Sally was speaking again. She sounded torn between being frightened and being thrilled.

"Don't joke about it!" someone scolded.

"It could be all too true."

Conjectures flew thick and fast until Alexander Stenn said, "Perhaps the Spanish officer just wants to look over the ship's papers. That would seem the logical course."

Nobody thanked him for the suggestion, which was too sensible to be attractive. It was far more fun to feed the fire kindled by the encounter and imagine the worst. Eventually, however, cold water was thrown on the flames when the Spaniard and Captain Windsor emerged once more. They were talking and actually smiling. Obviously, the visitor had been convinced that this boatload of gabbling girls was not a threat to the Spanish fleet, nor were the young ladies working in behalf of the Chilean Government. As the sun set over the western sea the *Continental* was finally granted permission to proceed to Lota for fuel and necessary supplies.

Lota proved to be a grubby little coal port, but apparently it was of enough importance to boast an American consul, who came out to the ship the next day to greet the girls and invite all the passengers to visit his house and gardens, an invitation Eliza found irresistible.

Rosie reinforced her inclination to join the excursion. "The old man won't give you a thought until we're at sea again," she promised. "Between you and me, I hear he's got *big* trouble, compared to which you're no more important than a pesky fly."

"What kind of trouble?" asked Eliza.

Rosie chuckled. "There's a six-week-old copy of the *Times* being passed around. It came in the mailbag waiting for us on shore. There's a news item in it that our leader is being sued for fraud by a New York couple named Thorne. The Thornes claim to have paid passage money for themselves and two children, but like some other unlucky souls they were left behind. Isn't Mr. Mercer the scalawag, though?"

After the word *mailbag* Eliza heard scarcely a word. If mail was being delivered, it could also presumably be sent. Immediately her thoughts flew to Thankful Turner.

Perhaps it was already too late. Perhaps Thankful had sent incriminating letters home from Rio. In Brazil, Eliza hadn't gathered courage to make a move, but now she realized she had been wrong in putting off an attempt to keep Thankful quiet.

"What's the matter, Eliza? You're white as a sheet." Rosie looked at her inquiringly. "Did you know the Thornes?"

Eliza shook her head. The name had meant so little that she had already forgotten it. Then, since she and Rosie were alone in the stateroom, she at last broke down and confided her secret fears. "Oh, Rosie, I'm a criminal. I ran away from the house where I worked. I stole money. Thankful Turner comes from Salem, and I'm afraid she might write home and say I'm on board. Maybe she already has!"

"How much money did you steal?" For once Rosie's gaze was earnest.

"Almost four dollars. To get to New York."

"Why didn't you save it out of your pay?"

"I didn't get paid," Eliza replied wretchedly. "Orphans don't, usually, when they're sent out from the asylum on their first jobs."

Rosie stood up with a sigh. "Well, we'd better go see her."

"We?"

"Sure. She could turn out to be a handful. Does she know about the money?"

"No, but she knows I ran away. I had to tell her, because she recognized me. You see, she was friendly with Amelia Endicott, the daughter in the house where I worked."

Rosie led the way to Thankful's stateroom and knocked on the door briskly.

"Who is it?"

"Rosie Brennan and Eliza Foster. May we come in?"

Without waiting for an answer, Rosie opened the door. Thankful, dressed for the garden party, was standing in front of a mirror adding finishing touches to her hair. "What do you want?" she asked, turning in surprise.

Eliza took a step forward. "Please, Miss Turner, I must ask you a question. Did you write home to anyone—anyone at all—that I'm on board?"

Thankful arranged a curl behind her left ear before replying. "I don't think so," she said with an air of boredom. "No, I don't think so. After all, why should I?" There were, she implied, more interesting things to put in her letters.

"Then please don't tell on me," begged Eliza, nervousness causing her to revert to the childish phrase. "I'm sure you wouldn't mean any harm, but it wouldn't do for Mrs. Endicott to know."

Thankful glanced over her shoulder, ignoring Rosie but appraising Eliza with a calculating eye. "What are you scared of?" she drawled insolently. "The police?"

As Eliza tried to control an involuntary shudder Rosie stepped between the two and met Thankful's eyes in the mirror. "I see some letters on your table, ready for mailing. The top one is addressed to Miss Amelia Endicott."

"So?"

"Miss Turner, I want you to listen and listen carefully." Rosie spoke in a tone that was meant to be offensive and succeeded. "If I find you've mentioned Eliza's presence on this ship to her or to anyone else in Salem, I'll forget my manners and knock your teeth in! That's not a threat. It's a promise. Do you understand?"

Thankful whirled around from the mirror. "How dare you—" she started angrily.

But Rosie gave her no chance to finish the sentence. "Come on," she said to Eliza, "let's shove off."

Backing into the corridor, Eliza collided with Alexander Stenn. "I'm just coming to fetch Miss Turner," he said. "Do you know if she's ready." Then he caught a glimpse of Rosie Brennan, and his eyebrows lifted. Obviously he considered her an unlikely visitor to be leaving the stateroom of a young lady of impeccable reputation.

Rosie read his expression correctly. "This was purely a business call," she assured him sweetly. "I think you will find Miss Turner quite ready, Mr. Stenn."

She took Eliza's hand and hurried her down the corridor, chuckling to herself. "Oh, dear," Eliza moaned, "I wish you hadn't—"

"Hadn't what?"

"Hadn't used such language."

"What would you want me to say? That I'd scratch her eyes out?"

"Rosie!"

"Look, dearie, the only important thing is that we shut her up. And I think I did. Did you see the expression on her face?" Rosie opened the stateroom door and shoved Eliza inside. "Miss Drummond left early to visit a missionary family," she said happily. "We can get dressed in peace."

While Eliza changed into her white dress and slipped into the clogs she had bought in Rio, hoping that nobody would notice her bare legs (the two pairs of stockings had long since worn out), her thoughts kept drifting back to Thankful. She hoped that Rosie was right, that Thankful would be effectively squelched, and although shocked by such rough threats, Eliza was sensible enough to be grateful.

"What's going on with Thankful and the professor?" asked Rosie, as she stood in front of the mirror pinning up her curls.

"She must truly believe that Mr. Stenn saved her life," replied Eliza.

"So she's giving him some attention at last. Well, let's hope he won't be disillusioned."

"Why should he be?" Eliza was impelled to ask, but Rosie was already at the door, listening for the signal that announced the last boat.

The consul's mansion, situated on a high bluff commanding a magnificent view of the Pacific, was in such contrast to the squalid village of Lota at its feet that to Eliza it looked unreal. To ascend from the unpaved streets and windowless huts of the town to the elegance of a residence surrounded by formal gardens was like walking from the orphanage directly into a palace. "Our diplomat does pretty well for himself," murmured Rosie in Eliza's ear, as they started on a tour of the flower gardens after being shown the house. Then she caught sight of Thankful and Alexander Stenn, strolling arm in arm ahead. "Begorrah, will you look at the professor and his ladylove!"

"Sh!" Eliza warned.

"But don't they look comical?" Rosie whispered. "She's half a head taller than he is, at least."

Granting that Mr. Stenn was short, Eliza still didn't like to hear him belittled. Although he had rarely spoken to her directly, she had come to respect his teaching ability and was beginning to admire him.

Rosie didn't enjoy flowers. Her interests lay entirely with people. As Eliza turned away to examine some magnificent roses she said abruptly, "I've had enough. I'm going back to the ship." And off she went, auburn curls bobbing, along the gravel walk that led to the gate.

Eliza wandered on until she came to a steep path leading to the beach. There was no reason to retrace her steps, so she picked her way downward, choosing a right fork as she listened to the sound of the surf and the cries of seabirds. She was quite alone.

The waves were rolling gently to the shore, and the sand was covered with shells, most of them broken.

Eliza went down to the tideline, kicked off her clogs, and walked barefoot, as she had not dared to on that memorable day in Rio. Turning over an occasional shell with a toe, she came upon a few that were intact. Once in a while she stooped to pick one up, wondering if she might ever find any as beautiful as those in Mrs. Endicott's collection. Most of these had lost their gloss and color.

Of all the shells she examined, Eliza kept only a few small ones. Holding them in the palm of one hand, she swung her clogs in the other. She suspected that in deeper water she might find more that were intact, but she had brought no handkerchief in which to tie her booty. For today this sampling would have to do.

A rocky promontory separated the curving beach from another closer to the port, but fortunately the tide was low and it was easy to wade around it. The water felt cool and silky on Eliza's feet, and she started to hum a tune Miss Stevens had been teaching her schoolchildren.

Then, on the far side of the bluff, she saw Thankful and Alexander Stenn, arms around one another's waists, walking unhurriedly in the direction of the dock. Feeling like an interloper, Eliza shrank back against the rocks and waited until they were mere specks in the distance. Then, brushing the sand from her feet, she slipped back into her clogs and followed.

She didn't pick up any more shells.

Chapter 10

When Eliza arrived back on board, the *Continental* was swarming with Chilean officers. Sally Marshall and Rosie were both holding court while Mr. Mercer wandered distractedly from deck to saloon, quite unable to cope with the situation.

Coal was being brought out to the steamer by lighters, which had been plying back and forth since early morning. Brawny stevedores hauled it aboard in jute bags, dumped it into the open hatches, then went back for more. By now a film of coal dust had settled everywhere, on deck, in the staterooms, even on the dining tables. The girls kept wafting their handkerchiefs over their skirts, which were taking on a grayish tinge, but the Chilean officers, undismayed, continued to pay them the expected compliments.

Because coaling was a slow process, the *Continental* lay over for more than a week, ample time for acquaintanceships to ripen into courtships and offers of marriage. Rosie acquired a particularly ardent admirer, a dark, mustachioed rancher reputed to be very rich. She flirted with him outrageously and allowed him to carry her off to look over his spreading acres. Shipboard gossip predicted that she would marry him, the lucky girl!

Eliza was torn between wanting the best possible future for Rosie and concern that she would lose her one good friend. She watched Rosie's dalliance with trepidation, reminding herself without success that she mustn't be selfish. The rancher came day after day, bringing flowers, bringing fruit, bringing sweets. Rosie accepted them all, dumped them in the crowded stateroom, and told Eliza she was having the time of her life.

That was plain to see. Breaking rules right and left, she was rowed in and out from shore in her admirer's skiff and was even seen dancing with him one evening on the moonlit hurricane deck.

Miss Drummond, horrified, reported the matter to Mr. Mercer as soon as she heard of it. Rosie was called on the carpet and properly scolded, but she refused to take Mr. Mercer seriously. As one of the paid-up passengers, she intended to continue to do as she chose.

Meanwhile, Eliza stood on the sidelines. Rosie involved in a romance became a stranger, not only self-willed but self-absorbed. Boisterously she joked about the Chilean's broken English, but delighted him by learning a few words of Spanish (most of them apparently naughty). Eliza could see that Rosie, although far from ladylike, knew how to charm a man.

On Saturday, the weekly market day in Lota, the cook went ashore with a boatload of girls. Concerned about an outbreak of scurvy, he was anxious to buy fresh vegetables. While he ordered huge baskets of produce sent to the ship, the girls haggled with the fruit sellers, becoming thoroughly irate as they realized that prices had doubled since the *Continental*'s arrival several days before. The trading soon developed into a shouting match, with neither side understanding a word the other said. The girls were easily the winners, snatching up their purchases and leaving whatever payment they chose, while the market women furiously screamed invectives in their wake.

A drenching rainstorm on Sunday kept both Rosie's rancher and the Chilean officers at bay, but the next evening they arrived on board in full force again. A few of the officers were even accompanied by their wives, who looked over the young ladies with disdainful eyes. The girls, shocked to find that their erstwhile swains were married men, retreated in confusion. Only those who had bona-fide offers, either of marriage or of a lucrative teaching post, began to pack up their belongings. For those who decided to stay, the Chileans promised to send a boat the next morning. Eliza, learning of the negotiations, was convinced that Rosie would go along.

Yet Rosie made no attempt to pack, either that night or the next morning, and when Eliza asked her directly whether she intended to marry she shook her head scornfully. "All the money in the world couldn't lure me into settling down in Chile," she said. "Live on a farm? Not Rosie Brennan. I'm a city girl, dearie. I'm looking for a spot with some *life!*"

Eliza was greatly relieved, but Miss Drummond greeted the news sourly. "You are a wicked woman," she told Rosie, "toying with a gentleman's affections, then playing fast and loose."

"How about him toying with *my* affections?" asked Rosie with a rippling laugh. "That's more to the point."

On the main deck a cluster of girls, surrounded by their luggage and a number of weeping friends, were waiting to go ashore. Coal was still being brought aboard and native marketmen were delivering produce to the galley. Confusion was piled on confusion when the Chilean boat, arriving at the hour promised, had to wait in line to pull alongside the ship.

Suddenly Mr. Mercer appeared, his face flushed, his red hair standing on end, and his black tie awry. He took up a belligerent stance on the gangway, then reached in his pocket and brought out a pistol, which he flourished threateningly. "Nobody," he commanded hoarsely, "is to make a move!"

Eliza, who had come on deck to see the excitement of the girls' leavetaking, stood cowed along with the rest. Mr. Mercer brandished his weapon in the air, shouting imprecations at the Chileans in the waiting boat while several girls in the projected landing party screamed.

"Over my dead body," shouted Mr. Mercer, "will

anyone take a passenger off this ship!" The girls wept and the Chileans argued and swore, but he held his ground.

In the midst of the hubbub, Captain Windsor arrived, quietly ordering the ladder to be drawn up. Although he looked thoroughly out of patience with Mr. Mercer, he didn't address him directly. "Be patient," he advised the distraught young ladies. "We'll get things sorted out by tomorrow. Everything will be all right."

Mollified by the promise that they could expect to be put ashore eventually, the girls dried their tears. The last of the coal was loaded, the market people returned to Lota, and the passengers regarded Mr. Mercer warily, wondering just how far he might have gone. Exhausted by the turmoil, most of the girls went to bed early, little dreaming that in the middle of the night the anchor would be hauled. By the time they awakened in the morning the *Continental* was far out to sea.

Apparently Mr. Mercer had told the captain that he had to leave despite the promise to the girls, but soon it no longer mattered. By midmorning the steamer was pitching so sharply in an angry ocean that most of those who had been deceived were too seasick to care.

Much of the native fruit brought aboard was over-ripe and quickly spoiled. Few of the girls paid attention to the cook's caution to wash all raw produce thoroughly, and dysentery replaced scurvy as a threat. In a stormy passage to a dingy Peruvian whaling port, where the ship stopped briefly, Rosie succumbed to the widespread flux and lost four pounds in as many days, both to her discomfort and her delight.

In time, everyone settled down again. The coal dust caused Eliza's laundry business to pick up, the ocean smoothed out, the girls resumed their flirtations with the *Continental*'s officers, and the romance between Thankful and Alexander Stenn became an accepted fact.

Although the general opinion was that they made rather an odd couple, Alexander gained considerable prestige as a result of the alliance. If Thankful, one of the most desirable girls on board, had discovered valuable qualities in him, he might be worth a second look.

Meanwhile, as the ship set a straight course for San Francisco, Mr. Mercer started to behave suspiciously. After hours spent shuffling through a portfolio of papers, he called one passenger after another to his stateroom and tried to cajole them into signing promissory notes for money he claimed to be owed. Some refused point blank, but meek little Miss Stevens and several others were taken in by his persuasive manner. After the briefest of interviews, Rosie flounced out of his cabin, furiously shouting that she'd see him in hell before she gave him a red cent. All in all, the gambit to find extra money proved unsuccessful and only succeeded in alienating some of the expedition members who had previously been loyal.

Few such diversions, however, occurred to relieve the tedium of the late March days. Not even a distant glimpse of land lent variety to the seascape. Roger Conant, having nothing interesting to write about, abandoned his notebooks and began paying court to one after another of the available girls. None seemed especially receptive.

Mr. Mercer, aware of the general restlessness, tried to invent some Bible-based games to interest his flock, but only the elderly and devout found them entertaining. The younger, gayer girls became more headstrong than ever, staying up long past midnight on a particularly warm evening when the almanac predicted a total eclipse of the moon.

Captain Windsor and Mr. Mercer stayed up too, policing the decks and trying to persuade the girls to get to bed, but discipline had become exceedingly difficult to enforce.

Miss Drummond considered the behavior of the young ladies scandalous and took to lecturing Eliza on the wicked ways of the world. (Rosie was obviously beyond redemption.) She spoke at length on her good fortune in being sent out to the Indians, whom she imagined as a simple, unspoiled people eager for conversion. Each day she sat at a sewing machine, stitching baglike calico dresses she called Mother Hubbards, a growing pile of which crowded the small stateroom still further.

"How do you know the squaws will like them?" Rosie asked.

"It isn't a question of liking. It's a question of decency," said Miss Drummond.

Rosie fingered the fabric of one of the garments.

"Pretty thin stuff," was her opinion. "They might do for summer, but not for mountain winters." She pretended to shiver. "It's said to get pretty cold in Washington Territory."

"There will be heat in the mission," said Miss Drummond comfortably.

"Aha, it's yourself you're thinking about, not the poor Indians," teased Rosie, but Miss Drummond made no effort to defend herself. Secure in her faith and in her principles, her expectations—as both Eliza and Rosie realized—were little short of glorious.

"She's in for an awful letdown," Rosie said to Eliza, when they were next alone. "The Indians are apt to be a terrible shock. She'd better marry the first man who'll have her, if you ask me."

"I doubt that Miss Drummond wants to get married," said Eliza. "I don't think she likes men much."

"Wait until a fellow comes along who waggles a finger in her direction!"

"Do you think one will?"

"With percentages what they are in the West, I'd say even Miss Drummond will be spoken for," Rosie replied easily.

"Then you'll be able to take your pick, Rosie."

"Sure, why not? *If* I decide marriage is my cup of tea."

Eliza was surprised. "What do you mean?" she asked, because marriage seemed to be the goal of all the young ladies.

Rosie shrugged. "I like the boys and the boys like

me," she admitted, "but I've got an itchy foot. I need
to move around."

"Will you go to work then?"

"I shouldn't be surprised." And she left it at that.

Day followed flawless day as the ship once more
neared the equator. The middle-aged and elderly dozed
on deck while Rod's "virgins" stirred up whatever
trouble they could find. Mr. Mercer rushed around
looking flushed and harried, making Eliza feel almost
sorry for him. Although he no longer seemed in the
least heroic, there was no denying the fact that his
luck had been wretched from the start. Had things
gone well he might not have turned out to seem such
a scoundrel, but things had gone very badly indeed.
Eliza now knew that from the day he had landed in
New York, to find notices of President Lincoln's death
posted everywhere, adversity had dogged his footsteps.
Failing to get help to secure a steamship, he had quickly
run out of funds and was forced to sign a contract with
a rich businessman who bought the *Continental*, then
charged Mr. Mercer a stiff fee for transporting his
cargo of girls to the West Coast.

Shipboard rumor claimed that men in Washington
Territory had forked over hundreds of dollars on the
expectation of being brought a bride. The girls themselves had also paid passage money, but even before
leaving New York Mr. Mercer was broke. In the meantime, he had manipulated funds, bought goods on
credit, failed to keep promises, lost three quarters of

the female passengers with whom he had hoped to sail, and now was losing his grip on himself. As the girls became more restless their leader became more irritable. Apparently he was realizing, belatedly, that robbing Peter to pay Paul was a dangerous ploy.

Captain Windsor eventually took charge of the worsening situation. When a group of islands were sighted about 700 miles west of Ecuador he decided to anchor for a few hours and give the girls a chance to work off some of their high spirits on shore. The excuse given was that the ship's engine needed some repair, but nobody was fooled for a minute. Captain Windsor, like Mr. Mercer, was simply at his wit's end.

The islands were called the Galápagos and were volcanic in origin. From the steamer they didn't present a very inviting appearance. Not a tree could be seen, not a bush or a shrub, only patches of long grass, apparently dead. The captain anchored on the north side of Charles Island, with which he was acquainted from previous voyages, and suggested that the men head for the interior to hunt game while the ladies could spend a pleasant interval walking the beach.

"That's excitement for you!" muttered Rosie, but Eliza was pleased by the prospect. She intended to look for shells.

When the captain's boat was lowered about ten o'clock in the morning a big party was ready and waiting. Most of the men carried guns, which caused a small panic among the girls, who professed to be frightened out of their wits. Roger Conant and Alexander Stenn, who possessed no firearms, came in for a certain amount of teasing. "Rod, you'd better stay with us," Sally Marshall said. "You can protect us from the wild animals the others will scare up in the bush."

"What bush?" asked Dr. Barnard. "Those rocks look as bald as my skull."

As it happened, Mr. Conant decided to go along with the men. "Just for the exercise," he said. So Alexander Stenn was left alone with the girls, who quickly held a conference and told him they didn't need his company either. Thankful clung to his arm for a moment, whispered something in his ear, then sent him off for a walk alone.

"What did you tell him?" asked Sally.

"The truth," said Thankful. "That everybody wants to go wading, but that no nice girl would think of taking off her shoes and stockings with a man around."

"Oh, piffle!" said Rosie. "What's wrong with bare feet?" She kicked off her shoes and peeled off her stockings before Alexander was more than fifty yards away.

"You are downright vulgar, Rosie Brennan!" scolded Sally, half serious.

"It's a heap more fun than being nicey-nice," Rosie retorted with a grin.

When Alexander was safely out of sight, the rest of the girls relaxed. Within a few minutes they were splashing about in the shallow water, playful as puppies. Eliza watched them for a few minutes, then put her clogs well above the tideline and wandered down the beach. Aside from the tracks of shorebirds in the sand and a few bright red crabs scuttling here and there, no sign of life existed.

But there were shells, and what shells! Again and again Eliza bent to pick up a new and stranger specimen, turn it lingeringly in her hand, then either discard it or add it to a growing collection in a bag she had brought along.

The best shells, as usual, were those that had not been bruised by rolling in the abrasive sand. They were down in the shallow water, through which Eliza waded, stepping carefully, peering down. She wished she had a book on shells and wondered if one had been written. Could it be possible that on this remote white beach she was picking up varieties never before seen by a human eye?

The shells came in many different colors, yellow, orange, white, pink, violet, and in dozens of different shapes. Each new discovery led Eliza on. She skirted rocks and jagged beds of lava, stopped to listen to a chorus of birds singing in the hills, and held her dress high so that she could get deeper into the water without getting wet. Above her head floated a swallow-tailed gull with red, webbed feet, but she saw only its shadow. Her eyes were down, always down, at the treasures in the turquoise shallows. In time, she reached a curving beach on which the sand was olive green, and later she came upon a strip of black sand tucked under great, overhanging rocks, but Eliza found the most fascinating shells on the white sand beaches.

Stooping to thrust an arm deep into the water, she let the hem of her frock slip out of her grasp, and it got soaking wet. Impatiently she took the dress off and flung it over a rock to dry. In her short orphanage shift she continued on, utterly absorbed, utterly alone. She was having a marvelous time!

How long she walked she had no idea. Then, happening to glance up, she saw that the sun was directly overhead. The girls had been instructed to be ready to return to the ship by lunchtime. Anxiously, Eliza started back.

She hurried past the black beach and the olive-green sand strip to the cove where she had left her dress. There it was, spread out like a striped moth on the rock. Clutching her precious bag of shells, she started to run toward it, then stopped with a stifled scream. Between her and the dress was a gigantic dome-shaped shell covered with horny, black-brown shields. It was as big as a small skiff and almost as broad as it was long.

Eliza backed off a few paces, not trusting her own eyes. The shell looked ancient and scarred, as if it had survived many battles. A green moss sprouted along its ridges, and a small bird lighted upon it for a moment, then flew quickly away. Rooted to the spot where she now stood, Eliza wondered whether she could be suffering from sunstroke. Surely, the shell had not been there when she had carried her wet dress to the rock. Then, while she gazed at it spellbound, the shell moved!

A reptilian head emerged, and dark oval eyes as big as hens' eggs stared at her expressionlessly. The creature rose slightly on scaly legs and short, club-shaped feet that might have belonged to a baby elephant. Ponderously, but far from slowly, it began to move toward her. Frightened out of her wits, Eliza abandoned the dress. She turned and ran.

"Hey! You're running in the wrong direction!" A shout from the rocky ledge that overhung the beach stopped her in her tracks. Alexander Stenn, his hands cupped to his mouth like a megaphone, was peering down at her through his spectacles. "Anything wrong?"

Eliza couldn't answer. She could only point. And while he clambered down the rough slope she moved even farther up the beach, out of the monster's line of march.

Alexander, followed by a hail of loosened stones, jumped to the sand. He saw the creature at once and gave a long, low whistle. "A giant tortoise! Are we in luck!"

"Be careful!" Eliza warned, her throat dry, her voice rasping.

"He won't hurt you," Alexander told her calmly. "Come closer. Isn't he remarkable? Must weigh three hundred pounds."

Eliza shuddered. "I don't doubt it." She hadn't budged an inch.

"Positively antediluvian," Alexander muttered.

"Ante—what?"

"Prehistoric. Very, very old." He was peering down at the tortoise in fascination. "Actually, turtles are among the world's oldest known creatures. They were here millions and millions of years ago, even before the dinosaurs." Reaching out, he tapped the shell with one foot. "That's called a carapace," he said. "Look how dented and blistered it is, Eliza. This fellow could have been hatched before the Revolutionary War."

Eliza didn't reply. She understood only part of what Alexander was saying, and even that part seemed like nonsense. "The Revolution was almost a hundred years ago," she murmured after a long interval.

"That's right." Alexander was strolling alongside the tortoise as though they were taking a walk together, while Eliza kept on backing away. "Know something?" he asked after a few moments. "These Galápagos tortoises are supposed to be able to carry a man on their back. Certainly they could carry a girl like you. Want to give it a try?"

Eliza gasped. "Are you crazy?" She had forgotten her manners entirely, along with her clothing.

"Maybe. But let's have some fun." Lightly Alexander leaped to the turtle's slippery back.

The snakelike head stretched and turned on its skinny neck, and the tortoise hissed. The toothless mouth opened, so that Eliza could see the horny edges of the jaws—jaws that could take off a man's hand. "Watch out!" she cried in alarm.

Laughing, Alexander slipped down to the sand again, avoiding the turtle's fleshy tail. Then he really looked at Eliza for the first time. "You'll get sunburned," he said. "Where's your dress?"

Chapter 11

Later, as Eliza smoothed some of Rosie's lotion on her sore shoulders, she marveled that she hadn't been embarrassed. To be caught half undressed would be an unthinkable predicament to any properly brought-up young lady, yet Eliza hadn't felt especially immodest. After all, the neck of the shift was higher than the necklines of most of the girls' dresses.

Besides, Alexander's matter-of-factness had eased the situation. He had been much more interested in the giant tortoise than in a slip of a girl whom he considered little more than a child. Eliza wasn't concerned that he would spread the story around. By now he had probably forgotten that they had met on the beach at all.

Eliza didn't forget, however. Alexander's daring had completely surprised her. Never again would she think of him merely as a teacher. He had revealed an unexpected quality—a sense of play.

By late afternoon, the repairs to the engine apparently completed, the captain was ready to sail again, but not before the hunters returned with their booty of wild game. A big tortoise was also brought aboard, almost swamping the boat that carried it. Ropes were dropped over the steamer's side, and it was hauled up by a dozen straining seamen, who positioned it helplessly on its back somewhere out of sight.

For a change, the cook looked positively cheerful. He roasted wild pig, which he served with Chilean cabbage, and after the game was gone he presented the passengers with delicious terrapin steaks.

Not until she had finished eating her dinner did Eliza learn that terrapin was really turtle, and by then it was too late to turn finicky. Besides, the cook subsequently made terrapin stew and terrapin soup, which he claimed rightly to be great delicacies. Eliza's education continued apace.

From the Galápagos to San Francisco, a trip of more than a fortnight, nothing more of interest was to be seen. The passengers became increasingly capricious, their tempers wearing thin. Shipboard friendships were made and broken rashly, from one day to the next.

Rosie could scarcely wait to reach California. "If I like San Francisco, I'm stopping off there," she told Eliza.

"For good?" Eliza quailed at the thought of parting from her protector.

Rosie shrugged, then asked with a wry smile, "Who knows?"

Eliza said, "I'd like to go see Harry's parents, if I can find out where they live."

"Talk to the purser," Rosie suggested. "He's supposed to notify the next of kin." Then she glanced at Eliza sharply. "Why put yourself through it?" she asked. "Harry's gone. His folks don't know you. And you're bound to be in for a bad time."

"I know," said Eliza. "I didn't mean I'd *like* to go exactly. But I feel I should."

"Why?"

"Because he would have wanted me to," Eliza replied.

Day followed tedious day, and by night the girls frolicked with such abandon that Captain Windsor joined Mr. Mercer in laying down the law. If their charges didn't obey the ten o'clock curfew, the two men rounded up the miscreants and led them to their staterooms. Mutiny among the passengers was no longer to be countenanced.

Rosie was so bored that she took up sewing again and made Eliza a coat out of a woolen skirt of which she had tired. Together the girls made a ceremony of casting Eliza's old coat into the sea. "Good riddance," Rosie cried.

The captain finally announced that the ship would go no farther than San Francisco, which caused great consternation until Mr. Mercer leaped to his feet and promised to send his party on to Seattle by bark or schooner. Some of the passengers were skeptical, and there was a good deal of muttering about previous promises having been broken. Still, there was little anyone could do.

At last, on a mild Tuesday in late April, land was sighted, and by afternoon the *Continental* was passing through the Golden Gate, the mile-wide entrance to San Francisco's harbor. Every able-bodied passenger on board, Eliza among them, was on deck to see the sights. Once Alcatraz Island was passed the girls had a good view of the city, which seemed to be built on great banks of sand and looked anything but promising. The hills were touched with green, but there were few trees to be seen. *Maybe Rosie will change her mind,* thought Eliza hopefully.

But Rosie wasn't in the least put off by the dismal picture. "Who needs trees?" she asked with a shrug.

"Don't get your hopes up, Rosie. The gold rush is over," advised Roger Conant, who was standing close by.

"So I've heard, Rod," said Rosie blithely, "but I've also heard that some of the chaps that struck it rich stayed on."

Eliza was still looking at the scattered trees. "I wonder what they're called?" she asked aloud. "Scrub oaks," the *Times* reporter told her. They seemed well named.

The ship came to anchor off Folsom Street Wharf, in a harbor crowded with more shipping than Eliza had seen in New York. There were clipper ships and steamers, lumber vessels and foreign traders manned by sailors who stared curiously at the *Continental's* cargo of girls.

Word was passed around that the ship would not dock until morning, to the great disappointment of the crowd of men waiting on shore. Some hired boats and rowed out to the steamer to beg for the privilege of coming aboard. They shouted at the girls and offered extravagant bribes, but Captain Windsor refused them, one and all.

Meanwhile, the crowds on the wharves increased as the news spread through the city that the *Continental* had at last arrived. Police were called out to keep the men in check, but not until darkness fell and the girls went below did the eager throng disband.

Some of the women were frankly terrified by the thought of the reception they were bound to get tomorrow. Appealing to Mr. Mercer, Miss Drummond made him promise to see her safely to a decent hotel. She prayed for a long time that evening, while Rosie crammed the last of her belongings into a bulging traveling bag and laid out the clothes in which she planned to go ashore.

Eliza, with next to nothing to pack, put her precious parcel of shells into her bundle-handkerchief and wondered if Seattle had a public library like Salem? Then the thought occurred to her that Mr. Mercer's university might have a book on seashells, if one existed. With a collector's enthusiasm she dreamed of being able to sort and label her discoveries. And someday, in an improbably golden future, she might even own a cabinet to put them in!

There was a knock on the door, which Rosie answered. Eliza had already climbed to the pipe berth, and Miss Drummond did not get up from her knees.

A junior officer stood outside. "Captain Windsor would like to see Whatsername, the laundry girl."

"Her name is Miss Eliza Foster, and I'll thank you to remember it," Rosie said.

"Is she here?"

"Yes, she's here."

"Then ask her to come down to the saloon, please," said the officer more politely. "As soon as possible."

Eliza swung herself down from the berth as soon as the door was closed. She was so accustomed to feeling threatened that her eyes grew round and apprehensive. "What do you suppose he wants of me?" she asked Rosie.

"Look on the bright side, Eliza. Maybe he wants to offer you a job."

"Oh, Rosie!" Slipping back into her clothes, Eliza tried to seem outwardly calm, but Rosie wasn't fooled.

"Want me to come with you?"

Eliza shook her head. After tomorrow, she was thinking, I won't have Rosie's support, so I may as well start doing without it now.

The captain was pacing up and down the almost empty room when Eliza slipped through the door. He looked around at once and said, "The purser tells me you were a friend of Harry Svenson's, the sailor who was drowned."

"Yes." Eliza whispered.

"His parents live on the outskirts of the city," Captain Windsor told her. "I'm planning to go break the news personally. Would you like to come along with me?"

"Oh, yes!" Eliza breathed. "Thank you, that would be ever so nice." She had always thought of the captain as something of a tyrant, but now she found herself looking up into the eyes of a tired, elderly man who had an unpleasant task to do.

Captain Windsor cleared his throat. "You may have heard that the first mate, Mr. Corrigan, could have been instrumental in causing Harry Svenson's accident."

"I saw the cut rope in the rigging," said Eliza, "and I know there was bad feeling between them." She bit her lip. "But I don't know why."

The captain shrugged. "There were a lot of little things, culminating in a quarrel over a woman."

"Over a *woman*?" Eliza's eyebrows lifted in shocked disbelief.

"Her name is Rosie Brennan," Captain Windsor continued quickly. "It seems the mate made a scurrilous remark about her, whether justified or not is beside the point. Young Svenson took offense and attacked him pretty roughly. Corrigan has been cooling his hot temper in the brig. The San Francisco police will take over tomorrow morning. There will be a trial, of course. But what I'm leading up to is this. The matter is one that would only trouble Harry's parents, so it would be kinder not to mention it."

Eliza agreed and said so, but she couldn't leave the captain without telling him one important thing. "Harry knew I was sleeping in a pipe berth in Rosie's stateroom. He also knew that she was my one good friend."

Captain Windsor looked into Eliza's eyes for a long moment. "Thank you," he said finally. "This helps me understand the circumstances far better than before." Then he drew himself up and resumed his former brisk manner. "I won't be able to get away from the ship until tomorrow afternoon. Mr. Mercer will see you to a hotel, with the rest of the girls, so I'll call for you there at three o'clock."

So there *would* be a hotel! That was good news. The more pessimistic girls had been predicting that Mr. Mercer would dump them all in the streets of San Francisco, despite his repeated assurances.

Eliza told Rosie and Miss Drummond at once that they need have no further fear of being abandoned, bag and baggage, on the wharf. Reacting in typical ways, Miss Drummond said, "My prayers are answered," while Rosie narrowed her eyes thoughtfully and muttered, "That'll give me time to turn around."

Breakfast the next morning was a sketchy affair, consumed while the *Continental* was edging up to the dock. Again there was a huge congregation of men waiting on shore—bearded miners in baggy trousers and boots, Mexicans in sarapes and sombreros, Chinese with long queues and straw hats like baskets worn upside down. Here and there in the crowd a Chilean called something in Spanish, and once in a while the broad brown face of a Hawaiian loomed above the other heads. Compared with the group of New Englanders that gathered on the Salem waterfront when a ship arrived home with rubber from Brazil, this jostling throng looked wild and unpredictable.

Mr. Mercer hurried ashore, fought his way through the crowd, and returned after an hour to announce, in his ponderous manner, that the International and Tremont House would be glad to accommodate his party. He cautioned the girls to stay close together when they went ashore, to keep their eyes lowered, and to hang on tightly to their possessions, as there might be pickpockets about.

"I will take the lead," he said, "as usual."

With the efficiency of a sheep dog harrying a flock of ewes into a pen, Mr. Mercer formed the girls into a wedge-shaped group and marched off at its head. The entire city of San Francisco seemed bent on seeing Mercer's belles arrive. Men and women lined the streets, leaned from upstairs windows, and peered from vantage points on top of wagons. The girls (even Rosie) behaved as sedately as anyone could have wished, but the men who had come to the dock were not put off. They formed a rear guard and marched along at the party's heels, following them all the way to the hotel.

Eliza was not exactly mistrustful, but she was disquieted. The environment was far rougher than she had expected, and Seattle, nearly a thousand miles to the north, was said to be even more primitive. In fact, the dismal condition of Washington Territory was described so graphically by the Californians crowding the hotel lobby that many of the girls were appalled.

Well-dressed ladies accompanied by their husbands had gathered in the hope of finding household help among the Mercer girls, and they swarmed over the arrivals like bees, buzzing with stories of the terrible conditions they could expect in the Puget Sound area.

"Why go on when you can do so well here?"

"Five dollars a week for a strong young lady who knows how to cook. My wife don't, I can tell you!"

"Six for the pretty one in the corner."

The proposals turned into raucous bargaining among the men, while Eliza, caught in the middle of the group of newcomers, lent an interested ear. Perhaps it *would* be sensible to stop off here, where money seemed to be as plentiful as the sand tracked in from the street.

While the overtaxed hotel staff tried to settle girls in the rooms hastily arranged for them, San Francisco matrons scrawled name and address on slips of paper and thrust them into any hand they could reach. Eliza found herself especially sought after, perhaps because she looked both poor and susceptible. One scrap of folded paper handed to her was heavy, and when she reached the dormitory to which she was assigned, she found that it contained a gold piece as a bribe.

Such openhandedness was utterly confounding to a girl raised in Massachusetts. Here, given to her by a stranger, was enough money to pay back her debt to Mrs. Endicott. San Francisco was El Dorado indeed!

Yet the view from the hotel window was far from

enticing. Grassy hills, mud flats, and a hodgepodge of wooden buildings that looked as if they'd blow away in a northeaster. Ugly, thought Eliza. So terribly ugly! If only there were more trees!

In the dormitory the girls twittered and fussed, vying for the cot with the best location, marking off their chosen territories with hand luggage, sorting out the offers made in the hubbub of the lobby, and making up their minds what to do. Sally Marshall had been tendered two proposals of marriage, written out on paper, by whom she didn't know. Waving them in the air, she climbed on a bed and offered to sell them, but her companions only laughed. They recognized, by now, that in this raw but rich city none of them need go begging. They need only make a choice.

Although she continued to be quiet and self-effacing, Eliza shared the sense of excitement that swept the others. She looked at the gold coin she had been given in renewed astonishment and wondered what Mrs. Endicott would think of such profligacy.

She wouldn't believe it, that's what! Eliza said to herself. Knotting a handkerchief around the coin, she looked for a place to hide it while she pondered the question of whether to search for the address and apply for the offered job.

Rosie would have stuffed it into the bosom of her dress, but Eliza's breasts were still immature. She knew only too well that the coin would find no resting place there. Of course, there was her bundle-handkerchief, but she couldn't carry it with her everywhere, especially not this afternoon when she went with Captain

Windsor to see Harry's folks. In the end she tucked the gold piece down the side of her left boot, and in time it settled under the arch of her foot, where it remained all day, more comforting than uncomfortable.

Rosie had not been lodged in the dormitory, nor did Eliza see her at lunch. The girls were led into the dining room like a class of schoolchildren, settled at long tables, and fed the cheapest meal the hotel could provide. Mr. Mercer, as their shepherd, urged them to disregard the curious faces peering in from the street, as well as all offers of employment. "Our destination is Seattle," he said in a deep, persuasive voice. "Seattle! Don't forget it. San Francisco is a city of vice and temptation. We leave here the moment I can book passage. Until then stay indoors out of harm's way."

To enforce his order, he stationed himself at the hotel door until the girls went upstairs. Only Eliza remained behind, and he scowled at her. "What are you doing here?"

"I'm waiting for Captain Windsor, sir."

"Nonsense. The captain is supervising the unloading of the ship."

"He said he'd call for me here at three o'clock," Eliza started to explain, but Mr. Mercer cut her off with a snort.

"What's come over you, girl? Are you daft or are you lying?"

"Neither, Mr. Mercer. He's—"

At that moment Eliza found the captain beside her, making further explanation unnecessary. "Where are you taking this girl?" roared Mr. Mercer at Captain

Windsor himself. "She belongs to my party, and I won't permit her to stay in this God-forsaken town."

Such a switch in attitude nonplused Eliza until she realized that Mr. Mercer was greatly afraid of losing any of his young ladies to the blandishments of San Franciscans. He had promised his Seattle backers to deliver more than twice the number he now commanded, so even the least of his ewe lambs had acquired value.

Captain Windsor, whose disenchantment with the expedition's leader was common gossip, replied as briefly as possible and grasped Eliza's arm, leading her out of the lobby and handing her into a waiting carriage. "Young fool," he muttered. "As if I care a rap where his flock ends up." Then he shoved aside a seabag, which Eliza realized was Harry's, that was crowding his feet. "Well, now let's be off."

The horse plodded slowly along Market Street and turned into a gravel road that led toward the hills. Eliza, overawed by the captain's presence, sat fingering the shell necklace Harry had given her and trying to figure out how she could be of help.

Gradually the landscape worsened. The houses gave way to shacks, the road to a cart track where a few stunted scrub oaks leaned against the wind. Eliza was saddened by such desolation, but Captain Windsor glanced around with interest. "The city is moving out and up," he said after a few minutes. "Someday it will be a splendid place, a real metropolis."

This opinion echoed Harry's sentiments, which now

seemed extravagant to Eliza. "Have you always lived in San Francisco, Captain Windsor?" she asked.

"Nigh on thirty years," replied the captain. "The best part of my life."

The driver of the carriage took another turning and pointed the horse along a street somewhat neater than the one they had just left. The houses were small, but they looked well cared for, and the sand that fronted them was raked.

"Here we are, sir."

The cottage before which the carriage stopped had a foreign appearance, whether because of the half curtains at the windows or the front door painted with a bright-colored design, Eliza couldn't be sure. "Ready, get set, go," muttered Captain Windsor, but he couldn't manage an encouraging smile.

Eliza, for her part, wished desperately that she hadn't come. She had no business here, standing before the house to which Harry had yearned to bring her. She wanted to turn and run.

However, Captain Windsor had already knocked, and the door was opening. A grizzled, red-faced man with a shock of unruly gray hair and direct blue eyes like Harry's stood inside, and from a room at the rear a plump woman in a long apron came forward. Neither looked at Captain Windsor directly. Their eyes were riveted on the seabag he was supporting with one hand.

Mrs. Svenson was the first to speak. "Our Harry. He's gone?"

The captain nodded. "I'm sorry to bring you such sad news, ma'am."

Her husband, who had been leaning on a cane, limped to the nearest chair. "How did it happen?" he asked with a strong Scandinavian accent. "He took sick?"

"No," said Captain Windsor with a shake of his head. "Somehow he fell from the rigging. Overboard. We searched for an hour, but we couldn't find him. It was a black stormy night."

"Drowned. I never figured Harry would drown. He was such a good swimmer, wasn't he, Mum?"

"A strong swimmer, yes," said Mrs. Svenson in a broken voice. Tears were sliding unnoticed from her eyes, and she was clasping and unclasping her hands.

Without conscious will Eliza went over and put her arm around Mrs. Svenson's shoulders. "Harry was a friend of mine," she said softly. "He was a fine young man."

In time, the captain introduced both himself and Eliza. "I thought you might like to hear from someone who knew your son better than I did. You see, a steamer the size of the *Continental* carries a pretty big crew."

"The *Continental* it was then? The ship of virgins? You heard tell of it, Mum. Sailed from New York."

"That's right," Captain Windsor said. "We've been at sea more than three months."

"Came around the Horn?" Mr. Svenson seemed to be asking questions in order to keep himself from thinking, from coming to grips with the stark knowledge that Harry was dead. His wife, on the other hand, allowed Eliza to lead her to the rear of the small, square room, where she lowered herself to a bench and wept unashamedly. "He was all we had," she said between sobs.

Eliza knelt at Mrs. Svenson's feet. "I want to tell you how very kind Harry was to me," she said, and she explained how they had become acquainted. "Most men would have turned me in as a stowaway, but he took pity on me right away."

"Of course he did," Harry's mother said.

"I used to hang laundry on the hurricane deck," Eliza went on. "We came to be friends. He wanted to bring me here to meet you—to meet his ma and pa, he said."

Mrs. Svenson blew her nose on a drenched handkerchief. "He did that?" She seemed to see Eliza clearly for the first time. "Did he ask you to marry him, miss?"

"No, but I think he meant to, when the time was right." Eliza wanted to be honest with the Svensons.

Harry's mother reached out and grasped Eliza's hands. "He was always looking for a good girl, a decent girl, not like the kind that roam the saloons downtown. It was time for him to marry, and we approved, didn't we, Pa?"

Mr. Svenson didn't hear. He was listening to the captain.

"Didn't we, Pa?" There was no answer.

"Listen, Eliza, you stay here with us. Like a daughter, I mean. We got enough to keep you, and Harry would have wanted that."

Eliza drew back and shook her head. "Thank you," she said. "You're very kind, like Harry. But, you see, I must go on to Seattle."

The statement came unbidden, a decision she had reached unknowingly, and while Eliza rode back into the center of the city at Captain Windsor's side, she didn't regret it. If only Rosie would come along!

Rosie, however, was still nowhere to be found. Nor did she turn up at the hotel for dinner, and although Eliza kept returning to the lobby at intervals until after ten o'clock, she didn't see her come in. Not until the next day at noon did she come across her, standing under the International and Tremont's sign while she talked with a stranger, a woman with hair bleached almost white who was smiling persuasively.

Eliza, who had been to the post office to inquire about buying postal-note stamps with her gold piece, went through the hotel door unremarked, then lingered in the lobby until Rosie appeared alone. Her breath smelt of alcohol, and she walked with a slightly rolling gate, which was not unnatural. Eliza found her own steps still trying to compensate for the motion of the ship.

"Rosie!"

"Oh, hello, dearie."

"Rosie, where have you *been*?"

"Out and around, seeing the town. It's a lively place all right!"

Eliza pulled her friend over to a green-plush sofa and sat down beside her. "Please, please! Don't stay in San Francisco. I'm sure Seattle will be much nicer!"

Rosie patted Eliza's knee sympathetically. "You're not going to miss me half as much as you think," she said gently. "You're a big girl now, honey. You've grown up in these three months. Besides, you'll do better on your own."

"No, I won't. I need you!" cried Eliza.

"Look, dearie, there's no use pleading with me. I'm staying here. Did you see that lady I was just talking to, the one with the diamond brooch pinned to her bosom?"

Eliza nodded.

"I just happened to run into her yesterday," said Rosie, "at a shop where I was buying stockings. One thing led to another, and this morning Flora stopped by to see if I'd like to work for her. She runs a real classy house and needs an extra girl."

Eliza couldn't stifle a gasp of surprise. "You're going to do *housework*?"

With one of her contagious grins, Rosie said, "Well, in a manner of speaking." She got up with a quick excuse. "I've got to go collect my duds."

Feeling almost as bereft as she had on the night Harry was drowned, Eliza knew that there was no use pleading. Nothing she could say would keep Rosie from walking up those stairs and out of her life. There was little hope that she would ever see her again.

Before she had gone five paces, however, Rosie turned and came back. Catching Eliza to her in a rough embrace, she bent and kissed her forehead. Then, in a choking voice, she said, "God, you're a sweet kid! Stay that way."

Chapter 12

Rosie Brennan was not alone in succumbing to the lure of San Francisco. By the time Mr. Mercer had made arrangements to send his party to Puget Sound on lumber vessels more than twenty others—schoolteachers, houseworkers, and maids mad to marry—decided to stay on. Sally Marshall was one of them, but Thankful found the town too rowdy for her taste. Besides, Alexander Stenn was going on to Seattle, and because his expectations were high Thankful was induced to anticipate it as the promised land.

Unable to pay the board bills at the hotel, Mr. Mercer delivered the *Continental*'s out-of-tune piano as security. Then (so the rumor went) he skipped out of town on the heels of the young ladies, in debt to everyone around.

Eliza found herself aboard the same schooner as Thankful and Alexander, a ship in no way geared to accommodate ladies comfortably. Thankful was appalled at the cramped quarters, and at the rough jokes the lumbermen made at the girls' expense. But once the sails were hoisted there was no turning back, and for nearly a month she endured "unthinkable conditions." She behaved like a princess in prison, keeping her nose in the air and her manners intact as she leaned on Alexander's willing arm and complained bitterly.

Eliza, reared to expect discomfort, made do quite nicely. She missed having books to read, but found the spring air pleasant and the coastline interesting. The food served to the passengers by a Chinese cook was strange and delectable, quite different from the hearty fare prepared routinely for the crew.

Still nested in Eliza's shoe was the gold coin she had received in San Francisco. The lines at the post office had been so long that she had abandoned the notion of buying postal notes and returned to her original plan of sending Mrs. Endicott the first money she earned in Seattle. In that way she would be discharging her obligation through her own efforts, not because of a stroke of sheer luck.

Whiling away the May days, Eliza took stock of her situation. She had no fear of not finding employment (San Francisco had been an eye-opener), but her dreams were beginning to take a new shape. At first, of course, she'd have to settle for housework, but after a time she was hoping to get more schooling—enough, perhaps, to enable her to teach.

From time to time she considered approaching Alexander to ask his advice, but he was so taken up with

Thankful that the opportunity did not present itself. The pair spent most of their waking hours together, quite oblivious to the rest of the passengers.

Finally, toward the end of the month, the schooner arrived in the headwaters of Puget Sound, a body of water so beautiful that Eliza's heart quickened with delight. The breeze was brisk, the sails full, and the shores were lined with immense forests of evergreens. The tops of the trees reached into the clouds, and when the sun broke through in the afternoon a great mountain range could be seen in the distance, with one soaring peak crowned with snow.

Standing alone on the sloping deck, her arm wrapped around the forward mast, Eliza felt weak with excitement. The land was what she had been hoping for —better than New England!—more glorious than anything she had ever seen. The sight filled her with unexpected vigor, a great desire to embrace the trees and the mountain, to make this country her own. Oh, Rosie, you were wrong, wrong, she cried silently. You shouldn't have settled for San Francisco. This is truly grand!

The Sound opened up like a great inland sea, and the schooner cut through the water like a homing bird. Now and then a fish leaped or a gull swooped, and here and there a little settlement of a few houses invaded the forest. But man had as yet left little imprint on this untamed land.

"Like what you see, Eliza?" Alexander had come on deck, and for once he was alone.

"Oh, yes," Eliza breathed. "Yes, indeed."

"Over to the right," he said, "is Mount Olympus. The one on the left is Baker. I've been brushing up on my geography."

"And way up ahead?"

"That's Mount Rainier, the third highest peak on this continent."

"Thank you, professor." Eliza didn't speak scathingly, yet Alexander was put off.

"I do tend to lecture. Forgive me. I should consider Mr. Mercer's bad habit and mend my ways."

"Not at all. I like to learn things," Eliza said.

"Out here I have a feeling there will be a lot to learn. It will be an entirely new experience, for all of us."

Eliza quite agreed. She wondered how Thankful would react to the grandeur of the scenery and the remoteness of Washington Territory. Everything was so different from tidy New England, her familiar world.

Thankful herself appeared at that moment. She had changed into one of her most becoming costumes and had the ribbons of a spring bonnet tied under her pretty chin. At once she grasped Alexander's arm for support. "Isn't this exciting?" she cried. "How soon will we be able to see Seattle?"

"It's just coming into view now," Alexander told her, "to the left up ahead." He pointed toward a place that looked to Eliza like a scar on the hillside.

"I mean the city," Thankful said.

"When inhabitants are counted in hundreds rather than in thousands, I'm not sure you can call it a city,"

Alexander replied. "It's more like a fast-growing town, I expect."

"Oh, dear." Thankful bit her lip. "I'm beginning to be rather frightened. I do hope everything isn't *too* strange." Then her eyes lifted to the snow-covered peak in the distance and she shivered. "What's *that?*"

Alexander repeated his lecture for Thankful's benefit, but she paid little attention. She seemed to find the mountains frightening rather than magnificent, and she kept straining to see the port toward which they were sailing in a following breeze. "Oh, dear," she sighed again, as the schooner drew closer to the docks. "It's even smaller than San Francisco, isn't it?"

"What did you expect?" Alexander sounded vaguely irritated.

"I don't know, but not this." Tears came to Thankful's eyes, brimming over as she searched in her purse for a handkerchief. "Why, it looks barely civilized!"

Eliza moved away. Thankful is living in the past, she thought, expecting a newer, more gracious Salem. In a way, Alexander seemed almost as naïve, looking forward to a university campus almost as inspiring as Harvard's. That they would both be disappointed Eliza felt sure, but she couldn't do anything about it. In contrast, to start (as she did) from nothing and to expect nothing was rather good. From down, everything was up.

And so were the hills of Seattle. Up, up, up! A jungle of stumps and scattered wooden houses, rising to what must surely be a glorious view of Puget Sound on one side and mountains on the other.

In a part of her mind, Eliza regretted the loss of the trees, but she remembered a precept of Mrs. Endicott's. "You can't make an omelet without breaking eggs."

The peekaboo sun had disappeared when the schooner finally docked in the afternoon. "Talk about a one-horse town," Thankful was raging. "A mile-high clearing in a forest, with two sawdust-filled streets. That's all it is!"

Alexander had eyes only for the university, a white, colonnaded building situated on a knoll. In his mind's eye, Eliza was sure, he saw it burgeoning, expanding, becoming the principal educational institution of the Northwest. At the moment, however, it looked more like a big square town house from Massachusetts, and apparently there were no students in the group that greeted the boat. Mr. Mercer, who had arrived earlier by brig, was waving cheerfully from the wharf, but the crowds of men who had greeted the *Continental*'s arrival in San Francisco were missing. Aside from squatting groups of Indians, the expected reception committee was few in number.

The few, at first glance, were unprepossessing: big, brawny lumberjacks who were chewing tobacco and standing with their hands in their pants' pockets as they watched the crew make the schooner fast. Here and there among them was a man in a jacket that matched his trousers, and one fellow in particular stood out from the group. He was tall, broad-shouldered, black-haired, with an Irish insouciance and a keen eye. His fawn-colored suit looked city-tailored, perhaps London-made, and with a trader's perspicacity his glance roved over the girls waiting to disembark.

Eliza saw his eyes stop on Thankful and watched a smile spread across his face. Too late, she thought. Thankful's spoken for by Alexander, or she will be soon. Then Eliza remembered Rosie's prediction that Thankful's sights were set higher than any of the men on shipboard. Well, time would tell.

Apprised of the schooner's arrival, a number of other townspeople were hurrying down the steep street to the dock. They looked like sturdy country folk and didn't frighten Eliza, but fear of strangeness swept the other girls like a cold wind. Where was the golden future Mr. Mercer had promised? Surely not here in this village of straggling two-story buildings. Only Alexander Stenn, with his eyes on the university knoll, and Miss Drummond, who was being welcomed by a soberly dressed missionary couple, seemed pleased.

"We've been sold!" Eliza heard a disappointed young lady mutter, while others, past coherent speech, burst into tears. Even Mr. Mercer was no longer at pains to be encouraging. "Go right up the street," he told the girls briskly. "Everyone is gathering at the Occidental Hotel."

Several passengers, concerned about the disposal of their luggage, lingered at the schooner's side, but Eliza trudged obediently up the hill with her bundle-hand-kerchief, weighty with the shells she had gathered, carried carefully in one hand. Along the way people stood singly or in groups, gazing at the Mercer girls in friendly curiosity. Young men nudged each other, old men grinned, and the few women who came out of the stores and houses stared at the crinolined skirts of Thankful and her companions with admiration or envy in their eyes.

Eliza, whose new coat was over her arm and whose short, striped orphanage frock was conspicuous among the girls in crinolines, caught the attention of a tall, spare woman with a shock of white hair piled haphazardly on top of her head. She was wearing a calico dress and sturdy shoes, and the expression on her face was kindly but businesslike.

"Could I have a word with you, please?" she asked.

"Certainly." Eliza stepped to the side of the road and looked up into the woman's face, youthful despite the white hair.

"My name is Sadie Harris. Miss Sadie, they call me, although I'm a widow. Are you looking for work?"

"Yes," said Eliza.

"Housework?"

Eliza nodded, and a smile flickered across her lips. That would have been easy to guess, she knew, from her shabby clothes.

"I run a boardinghouse, and I need someone to help me," said Sadie Harris. (She didn't use the terms *girl* or *housemaid*, Eliza noticed.) "Business is good—almost too good—and I can't handle the place all alone."

"What would the work be?" asked Eliza, as she tried to size up this prospective employer.

Miss Sadie chuckled. "Just about everything. Cleaning, laundry, helping with the cooking, waiting on table. You'd work right along with me."

"Where would I live?"

"There's a small room opposite mine, at the back of the house. The furnishings aren't much, but it's comfortable in the winter and it has a lovely view."

Eliza smiled, beginning to like Miss Sadie, who had touched a responsive chord in remarking on the view. "How much do you pay?"

"Three dollars a week."

Eliza drew back. "I've been told that in Seattle I might expect four," she said after a moment.

Miss Sadie threw back her head and laughed. "That scamp Mercer! He'd promise the earth with a ribbon around it. Schoolteachers get four dollars a week."

Eliza said, "Oh."

"Come look at the place, anyway," Miss Sadie invited. "It's right across the road."

The building to which she led Eliza was larger than most of the other houses but no more elegant. There was a front porch with a pitched roof, a row of evenly spaced windows on each of two floors, and an entrance hall that led to a sitting room, which also seemed to be used for dining, since there were two trestle tables set up at one end. The kitchen, at the rear, was very simple, with a scrubbed board floor and several black iron pots simmering on a stove. Miss Sadie took Eliza up a back stairway to the second floor, where she opened a door to a small oblong bedroom that contained a cot, a chair, some open shelves, and a clean blue-and-brown braided rug.

"Come look!" Miss Sadie said. "When folks complain about the hills here, we say, 'Ah, but the view!' "

The vista was indeed lovely. The lively waters of Puget Sound were backed by the Olympic Mountains, with forests of deep green clinging to the lower slopes. Still, how often would she—or Miss Sadie for that matter—have time to stand and admire the scenery? Eliza's practicality had been learned in a hard school. And she wondered why Miss Sadie didn't question her experience? Did she assume she was untrained?

"I've worked before," Eliza said, turning from the window, "in Salem, Massachusetts. I was a housemaid for Mrs. Endicott for three years."

Miss Sadie stifled a gasp. "But you're so young!"

"I'm sixteen," said Eliza proudly. "I went to the Endicotts' from an orphanage before I was twelve."

"Did you?" Miss Sadie spoke as if she were bargaining for time. After a moment or two of thought, she said, "Tell you what. You start at three dollars, but I'll raise you to four after a month if you're satisfactory. Is that a deal?"

"Four dollars in hard money?"

"Hard money if you like." Miss Sadie grinned. "You sound like one of the loggers. They don't trust paper money any more'n you."

Eliza put her bundle-handkerchief down on the unmade cot. "My name is Eliza Foster," she said. "Do you want me to start right now?"

"Gosh, that would be great," Miss Sadie said. "The bathroom's at the end of the hall. Come down to the kitchen when you've washed up. By the way, I forgot to mention that Sunday will be your day off."

A day off each week? Eliza could hardly believe her ears. She felt sure that she hadn't made a mistake in coming to such a quick decision. No matter how hard she had to work six days, the lovely seventh would be all her own.

Chapter 13

When Miss Sadie rang the dinner bell, sixteen men gathered at the two trestle tables. Most were in shirt sleeves, with the cuffs rolled up above their elbows, but a few wore conventional dark suits. "Salesmen," whispered Miss Sadie to Eliza. "In town for a couple of nights."

She was dishing up supper in the kitchen, great bowls of beef stew, potatoes, and pickled beets. Bread and butter were already on the tables, along with pitchers of milk and water. "Shall I start passing?" Eliza asked.

Miss Sadie looked surprised. "We don't pass here. Nothing fancy. Just divide up the dishes between the two tables. Put the stew down one end, the vegetables down the other. The men will help themselves."

When Eliza appeared in the doorway with a steaming serving bowl, the boarders stopped talking and stared at her as if they'd never seen a girl before.

"Well, I'll be—"

"Where did you come from?"

"I've got it! One of the Mercer girls."

"Not likely, Joe. They're too hoity-toity—"

"Fellows," said Miss Sadie, as she came in from the kitchen with a second bowl of stew, "meet Eliza Foster. She's going to help me feed my hungry hordes."

One of the salesmen got politely to his feet, then sat down quickly when the others turned to look at him.

"Evenin', Miss Eliza," said a brawny young man in a plaid shirt.

" 'Eliza' will do," said Miss Sadie, "although it's nice to hear a lad with manners for a change."

"Hey, what *about* Asa Mercer and his female pioneers?" asked a man who was helping himself to a great mound of potatoes. "I hear they've actually landed. Is that a fact?"

"Yup. They're at the Occidental."

"Better walk up and have a look-see, hadn't we, Joe?"

"Hey, Pete, you on the marry?"

"Not me, lad!"

"Cost you three hundred bucks if you want to pick a posy from that bunch," Joe remarked. "I know two fellas who paid cash money to Asa before he left town last year. He'd better deliver, I'm telling you!"

An older man put down his knife and fork. "I don't know what Mercer meant by bringing all those women up here. There's nothing for them to do."

"I hear most aim to be schoolteachers," said the young man in the checked shirt.

"That's just a cover-up," the older man said. "Most aim to marry, mark my words."

"Well, that shouldn't be hard."

"Not if they'll settle for life on a prairie farm or somewhere in the backwoods."

As she replenished the bread plates, Eliza listened to the conversation with growing concern for the girls who had come out to the Northwest with such high hopes. Here was the other side of the story for fair! Most of the girls were equipped to do nothing but find a husband, preferably rich. And as their dreams died they would have to make do with any man available.

Clearing the table as the men lit pipes or cigars and sauntered off toward the hotel, Eliza began to savor her own good fortune. Within hours of landing in Seattle, she had a job, a place to sleep, and the prospect of being able to support herself for as long as she could work for a living.

"Hungry, Eliza?" asked Miss Sadie from the kitchen sink.

"Sort of." Eliza didn't like to admit that she was always hungry, that the rich beef stew smelled heavenly. Probably such fare wasn't meant for her.

But Miss Sadie laid places for two at a small table by the kitchen window and ladled out fresh stew from the steaming pot. "We'll eat together," she said. "And don't forget, if you should be dishing up, always save plenty for us."

A greater contrast to life at the Endicotts' could not have been found, decided Eliza, as she sat opposite her employer. Miss Sadie was flushed from the stove, her hair was tumbling untidily from its pins, and she was obviously tired from a long day's work, but her eyes were shining. "They're a good lot, by and large, my boarders," she said contentedly. "A little rough at the edges, but then so am I."

"Do they *all* live here?" asked Eliza.

"Lord, no. I can only sleep ten. The rest stay at rooming houses and come for their meals. Sometimes, but not often—so don't get scared!—I've served as many as twenty."

Eliza wasn't scared. Wrapped in the warmth of the cluttered kitchen, she felt more at ease than ever before in her life. When Miss Sadie asked her how she happened to have come on the Mercer expedition, she told her the truth, even admitting the theft of Mrs. Endicott's house money. "The minute I've earned enough, I'll return it in postal notes," she said, pleased that she had learned the proper system for mailing currency.

Miss Sadie accepted her explanation without comment. She was more interested in Eliza's account of Mr. Mercer's visit to Salem than she was in her means of escape. "They say he can charm the birds right off the trees if he feels like it. Is that so?"

Eliza nodded. "He's a remarkable man, full of great ideas, and very convincing." She didn't want to say that the girls had also found him dishonest and hypocritical.

"Big ideas, that's Mercer. Take the university."

"What about the university?" Eliza asked quickly.

"Well, it's there. That's about all you can say for it." Miss Sadie pushed back her chair. "Let's get these dishes cleaned up. Then I'll find you some sheets and towels, and you can turn in early, if you like."

Although she wasn't sleepy, Eliza went to bed as soon as the kitchen was tidied. On the last leg of the journey west she hadn't worked at all, and she was thoroughly rested. More than anything, she would have liked to walk up to the hotel and see how the other girls were faring. The prospect of encountering Mr. Mercer held her back, however. Out of sight, she also might stay out of mind.

At breakfast the next morning Eliza got the news secondhand, by listening to the boarders' conversation. She gathered that things were at sixes and sevens at the Occidental, with young ladies milling around the halls, mountains of luggage piled on the board sidewalk, Indians peering in every window, all of the bachelors in town taking stock, and a number of backwoodsmen and truck farmers sleeping in their buckboards until they could get a word with Asa about the brides they had bargained for.

Because the Occidental was far too small to harbor so large a crowd, a number of generous Seattle people had opened their doors to receive some of the strangers. Families were promised houses rent free until they could get on their feet, girls were offered rooms until they could find employment, and everyone was very kind and welcoming.

Predictably, most of the young ladies refused to leave Mr. Mercer's protective wings until he could make some of his promises good. They turned down proposals of suitors named Humboldt Jack, Lame Duck Bill, Whiskey Jim, and Bob-tailed Joe indignantly. Instead of willing brides, the men from the hinterlands who had paid on the barrelhead found instead a clutch of unhappy Eastern women whose pioneer spirit didn't extend beyond the hotel steps.

Unable to claim their prizes, the farmers became surly. As one of the boarders said, they had to be home at sundown to milk the cows and feed the pigs. That left no time for courtship. It was now or never to get married, so far as they were concerned.

Later in the day Eliza discovered that some of the more desperate young women had decided to take their chances. Several buckboards departed with a bride aboard, and although sometimes her age was a disappointing thirty-five rather than twenty, a woman was a welcome thing.

As she swept rooms, changed beds, and soaked sheets in hot water generously spiked with lye, Eliza tried to imagine what Thankful and Alexander might be doing. From the upstairs front windows she could see the cupola on the university building, and she wondered whether Mr. Mercer had provided accommodations for his new teacher, or if Alexander was rattling around at the Occidental with the rest.

Eliza also wondered whether Mr. Mercer had missed her yet and knew that sooner or later she would have to approach him, tell him where she was working, and try to come to some arrangement about her enormous debt. When, in the early evening, she

saw him strolling down to the waterfront with Mr.
Conant, she ran out to the road and said, with new-
found resourcefulness, "Excuse me, but I think you
ought to know I've taken a job."

Mr. Mercer seemed distracted. He looked at her as
if he couldn't place her, then said, "Oh, Eliza, is it?
A job where?"

"At Miss Sadie's boardinghouse, sir. Right over
there."

"Oh, well, that's good. You wouldn't like to marry?"
Eliza flushed. "No, I would not."

"Too bad, but so be it." Mr. Mercer would have
walked on, but Eliza stood determinedly in his path.

"What do you expect me to do about the rest of
the passage money?" she asked, well aware that she
had paid him less than a hundred dollars.

At this point Roger Conant caught her eye and
shook his head in warning, but he needn't have feared.
Asa Mercer was so swamped by really big financial
problems, with lawsuits pending in New York and
San Francisco, debts running into the thousands, and
a growing feeling of hostility among those who had
invested in his expedition, that the prospect of extract-
ing a dollar or two a week from an impoverished
housemaid no longer seemed important. "Don't
bother me, girl," he said, and walked slowly on.

Eliza stood in the road until the two men, walking
downhill toward the waterfront, were out of sight. She
could scarcely believe her reprieve. Was she truly free
of the obligation to save money from each week's
wages to hand over to Mr. Mercer? Breathing a tremu-

lous sigh of relief, she finally turned and went back indoors. For the first time since her journey had begun she felt positively lighthearted.

The next few days passed quickly. Eliza worked hard, but Miss Sadie worked even harder, and a comradeship grew between the two that lightened their menial chores. Although Eliza never left the house, she was fascinated by the passing scene. "Everybody in Seattle goes by here sooner or later," Miss Sadie claimed, and pointed out the more colorful local characters.

"That's Henry Yesler," she said one morning. "Don't he look glum and tightfisted, though? He owns the sawmill down on the waterfront, and he's said to be one of the richest men in town."

"Look, Eliza," she called at another time. "See the old fellow with the big grin. That's Doc Maynard, our most prominent citizen. He keeps the trading post, and he's generous to a fault. Even gave Yesler the land for his mill, I've heard tell. One of Doc's best friends is Chief Sealth, of the Duwamish tribe. It's for Chief Sealth that Seattle is named."

Miss Sadie could distinguish the Indians by tribe. "He's a Muckleshoot," she'd say, or "That pair coming around to the kitchen door are Nisquallis. They bring me sockeye salmon once a week."

Fresh sockeye salmon turned out to be the best fish Eliza had ever tasted. Miss Sadie taught her how to clean them and bake them slowly in the oven, basting them in their own juices, and when Eliza took the first bite of the firm pink flesh, she rolled her eyes upward and sighed, "Mmm! I've never tasted anything half so good."

When Sunday morning came, Eliza helped with breakfast, then started off happily to explore the town, turning up toward the hills rather than down toward the waterfront. She passed the Occidental Hotel, a white wooden building sleeping under the low-hanging clouds. A muddy avenue fronted it, and from a steep side street a bridge led to the upper story. Nobody was to be seen at this early hour except a young lad in a long apron who was busily sweeping the front steps.

Although it wasn't actually raining, the air was misty and the June day was damp and cool. From time to time Eliza stopped, either to look back at the Sound, where an Indian was paddling his canoe toward an invisible shore, or up at the stump-cluttered hills where new houses were under construction. She liked what she saw. People out here were starting from scratch to build a city. The land belonged to anyone who could stake a legal claim to it, and there was plenty of space left for additional homesteaders.

On this first morning of exploration Eliza had a destination. She was heading toward the university building, standing on its knoll above the muddy streets. From the Sound it had looked handsome, and even on closer inspection it was quite impressive, if a little lonely, with its pillars and churchlike cupola. For Miss Sadie the university was a symbol of Seattle's struggle to become more than another mill town, but for Eliza it was a monument to the learning she so much admired. Besides, the university must have a library, and in the library she might find a book about seashells. Or so Alexander had led her to hope.

Of course, on Sunday—especially a summer Sunday —the university would undoubtedly be closed, but Eliza was drawn to it nevertheless. Miss Sadie had told her that Seattle doors were never locked, so there was a chance she might even be able to get inside.

Playing a game, pretending she was an entering student, Eliza went up the steps and stood for a moment looking at the tall columns. Then she went to the door and turned the handle experimentally. Miss Sadie was right. The door swung inward, and she stepped over the threshold into a big, empty entrance hall.

There was an office and a reception room but no sign of a library. Eliza tiptoed along the hall and glanced in at a couple of classrooms, with blackboards and fine new desks for the students who would doubtless flock here in the fall. She imagined Alexander standing before a class and lecturing (about what she couldn't conceive), and she understood why he wanted to be part of such a splendid project.

There was one more door at the end of the hall, and it wasn't ajar like the others. Timidly, because Eliza didn't want to surprise a caretaker, she pushed it open to see if this room might at last be the library. It was just another classroom, however, with one important difference. Seated at the far end of the room was a young man with his elbows on a desk and his head cradled in the palms of his hand. Although he was facing away from her, Eliza knew at once he was Alexander. She walked quietly down an aisle and stood at his shoulder for a long moment before he became aware of another presence in the room and slowly turned his head.

"Eliza," he said, not so much in surprise as in acceptance. "What are you doing here?"

"I was looking for the library," she replied, not that it mattered any longer. The expression of utter desolation in Alexander's eyes drove everything else from her mind.

Uncertain what to do, Eliza finally ventured, "You look sad. Is anything wrong?"

"Everything," said Alexander gloomily.

"What do you mean, everything?" Eliza found herself wondering whether Thankful was the cause. "Would it help to talk about it?"

Alexander shook his head. Then, in an abrupt change of mood, he sat back and flung his arms wide. "Look at this place!" he cried, almost sobbing. "It's an empty shell!"

"But it's summertime," Eliza said soothingly. "What can you expect?"

"I can expect nothing," Alexander raged, getting to his feet and storming up and down the room. "Nothing now. Nothing in the future. Asa Mercer claimed there were ten students when he left and predicted that the number would grow to fifty before he got back. Instead, there are none. And if there's a boy in all of Seattle with a high-school education I'll eat my shirt!"

At least he's angry, thought Eliza. That's better than being so woebegone.

"Do you realize what I'm saying, girl? Do you understand that there's nobody qualified for college in this whole wretched town? I've spent everything I owned to get out here on the assurance of a university teaching job, and now there's nobody for me to teach!"

Eliza stood with her hands clasped in front of her, wishing she could comfort him, but she understood Alexander too well to try. He was utterly shattered, beyond the help of anyone but himself. Mr. Mercer had obviously cheated Alexander Stenn, as he had cheated so many others, but there was no use crying over spilt milk, and she told him so.

Then Eliza also spread her arms wide, but not in a gesture of pushing space away. She was bringing everything she could envision into her grasp—the rude stumps she could see through the window, the energetic townspeople who slogged up and down the unpaved streets, the unparalleled opportunity the West offered.

"Just think," she cried, "we're here! Here in the most exciting place we've ever been in our lives. Don't give up in despair. *Do* something about it!"

Eliza knew at once that her enthusiasm had been ill timed. She attracted Alexander's attention, but only to the extent of making him glance at her and mutter, "We?" Then he turned his back and went over to the window, where he stayed until she left the room.

Going out of the building, which now seemed as bereft of purpose as Alexander, Eliza continued to trudge uphill and downdale until she came within sight of a great inland lake, but the zest had gone out of her excursion. Although she scolded herself for letting Alexander's discouragement affect her own state of mind, there was no help for it. Dutifully she ate the sandwich she had brought along, but shortly after noon she turned back.

The Occidental Hotel, which Eliza had found so quiet in the early morning, was now filled with noise and activity. Farm wagons were pulled up at the side of the road, the horses tied to hitching posts. Young women were coming and going through the doors, some of them stopping to talk to men who stood on the shallow steps or in the shelter of a porch roof. Eliza recognized several of the Mercer girls and was glad to see that they didn't seem downhearted. From the dining room came the rattle of plates and cutlery, and from the upstairs windows, open to the mild June breeze, came a medley of feminine voices sounding as if they had been transported straight from the *Continental*.

Nostalgia, threaded with curiosity, made Eliza wish she could be with the girls long enough to discover their plans. Who, she wondered, had married already, and who were being courted by the men gathered on the porch? She suspected the young widows had been spoken for quickly, while the plainer, middle-aged spinsters might have to wait until the fresher blossoms had been picked.

A carriage drawn by a matched pair of chestnuts swung around the corner and pulled up close to the hotel steps. The driver, springing clear of the muddy road, ran up to the porch, strode through the door, and returned a moment later with a girl on his arm.

Thankful Turner, smiling sedately and twirling an unopened parasol, was handed into the carriage by the black-haired man in the fawn-colored suit who had caught Eliza's attention at the dock. Today he was dressed in pearl gray with a chamois-colored vest, a costume equally elegant. In a proprietary manner he opened Thankful's parasol and arranged it so that she would be sheltered from the fitful sun. Then he took up the reins, slapped them on the horses' rumps, and drove uphill within a few feet of where Eliza was standing.

The carriage passed so close that mud from the wheels spattered her dress, but Thankful didn't turn her head to look at the damage. Once more, to the young lady from Salem, Eliza apparently had become invisible.

Two men in their twenties, dressed in Sunday clothes, banged out of the hotel door and came down Occidental Street as Eliza walked on. "Courtney Alsop," one of them said, as he chewed on a toothpick, "sure has a glad eye for the gels."

"He's found himself a winner this time," said his companion enviously.

"What do you mean—this time?"

"Don't you remember the last one, that pretty Indian squaw?"

"Can't say I do," said the man with the toothpick, as he brushed past Eliza.

"She was a winner too, in her own way." His friend chuckled.

"'Cawtney.' This new girl calls him 'Cawtney.' Is that a New England accent?"

Eliza didn't hear the answer. Having reached the boardinghouse, she went around back to scrape the mud off her shoes before going inside. Miss Sadie was seated at the kitchen table, drinking coffee. "You're back early," she said.

Nodding, Eliza told her, "I went as far as a big lake."

"That's Lake Washington. Someday, if business gets slack, I'll take you fishing there."

Fishing sounded to Eliza like a masculine sport, but she didn't say so. Under Miss Sadie's tutelage it might be fun.

"There's coffee on the stove. Pour yourself a cup."

"Thank you." Eliza came back to the table with a steaming earthenware mug and asked, after she had taken a sip, "Miss Sadie, do you know a man named Courtney Alsop?"

"Sure do. Handsome as a hawk and wild as a March hare. Black Irish and bound to make a fortune out of the building business, people say."

"Does he live in Seattle?"

Miss Sadie nodded. "Built himself a fine house up on the outskirts of town. Now he's looking over the

Mercer girls, I hear, aiming to find a bride if there's one among them who'll come up to his high standards."

"I think one of them has," said Eliza.

"Really? Tell me about her. I love gossip, when I have time for it."

"Her name is Thankful Turner," stated Eliza.

"Thankful? That's a peculiar name."

"Not in New England. We have lots of names like that. Prudence, Charity, Devotion—"

Miss Sadie grinned. "Get back to Thankful."

"She comes from Salem, same as I do," Eliza said. "Only Thankful is very well brought up and extremely pretty, so she was courted by all the ship's officers and one passenger in particular, a young man engaged to come out as a teacher at the university."

"The university with a faculty of one, Asa Mercer," muttered Miss Sadie. Then she asked, "Is the teacher rich?"

Eliza shook her head. "He's quite poor."

"He'd better go see Henry Yesler," Miss Sadie suggested. "I hear he's looking for a bookkeeper."

Eliza tucked this bit of information away in her mind as she mused aloud, "I don't think Thankful would like being married to a bookkeeper."

"If she's as pretty as you say she is, you won't have to worry," predicted Miss Sadie. "My bet is that Thankful will be mighty thankful to become Mrs. Courtney Alsop before the month is out."

Chapter 14

One of the salesmen boarding at Miss Sadie's left for San Francisco on a bark Monday morning, so Eliza was instructed to clean and air his room thoroughly. She was making up the bed with fresh sheets when Miss Sadie came to the door. "We've got a new roomer," she said. "Eliza, this is Mr. Stenn."

Alexander, who was carrying a heavy portmanteau in either hand, let both bags fall with a thud. "Eliza! What are you doing here?"

"That's the same question you asked me yesterday," Eliza said. "I'm working, as you can see." She drew herself up and looked him straight in the eye, trying to conceal her pique. Alexander had been so self-pitying Sunday morning that it hadn't entered his head to ask how she was getting along.

"Yes, yes, that's good." There was no enthusiasm in Alexander's voice. His thoughts were still turned inward.

"Miss Sadie, this is the teacher I was telling you about," Eliza said.

"Well, Mr. Stenn, you made a lucky choice among our several boardinghouses. You'll be among friends."

Eliza didn't see Alexander again until she served the boarders' supper. Sitting near the end of one of the tables, he was looking desperately unhappy. The other men, who were friendly enough at the start of the meal, tended to leave him alone by the time Eliza brought on the dessert.

"Your young man's sure got a poor-me look," said Miss Sadie, when she was drying the dishes Eliza washed.

"He's not *my* young man," raged Eliza, furious at Alex because he had allowed himself to be seen in such a light.

"Why don't you tell him about the job at Yesler's. He paid his board and room for a week in advance, but a week goes by pretty fast."

"All right, I will." Eliza dried her hands and marched into the front room, where Alexander was moping by a side window. "Miss Sadie says Mr. Yesler, who owns the sawmill, needs a bookkeeper. You may want to look into it."

Although he didn't change expression, Alexander said, "Thank you. Thanks a lot," and the next morning he disappeared after breakfast in the direction of the waterfront. He didn't come back until after the five o'clock whistle blew, and when he appeared at supper with the news that he had gotten the job, he looked slightly more cheerful. Eliza noticed that he even contributed a few remarks to the general conversation, although he certainly wasn't talkative. His behavior reminded her of the first days on shipboard, when his only companion was Roger Conant. Alexander seemed once more determined to keep himself apart, and although Eliza longed to inquire about Thankful, she didn't quite dare. Alexander might think she was presumptuous.

Good manners, however, demanded that he thank Miss Sadie for suggesting the job at Yesler's, so during the evening, after most of the boarders had wandered off to one or another of the dozen grog shops near the dock, he came to the kitchen in search of her.

Eliza had brought down some of the shells she had collected on Charles Island, spreading them out on the scrubbed table for Miss Sadie's inspection. "If only I could learn more about them," she was saying. "If only I could find a book!"

Alexander didn't linger. He expressed his appreciation to Miss Sadie politely, barely glanced at the seashells, and left.

"Unsociable cuss," commented Miss Sadie in an undertone.

"Not always. He was kind to me on the ship, in spite of the fact that he was an educated man, while I—" Eliza broke off and frowned, then said, "He's had a terrible blow, because he was looking forward so much to teaching."

"Then he ought to start a preparatory school."

"A what?"

"A school to prepare boys for college. In four years he'd be ready to move up to the knoll."

Eliza said, "That would take money."

"Plenty of money around if you go looking for it," replied Miss Sadie. "Doc Maynard's ready to promote anything that will help Seattle, and Doc could find other backers. Some of the first settlers have sons and want to see them educated. That's why the university's *there*."

Eliza thought Miss Sadie's advice over at her leisure, but it wasn't until the next Sunday that she mentioned it to Alexander. Then, on an impulse, she approached him right after breakfast. "Have you seen Lake Washington yet?" she asked.

"No," said Alexander shortly.

"Oh, you must! It's an inland lake, long and lovely. This is my day off, so I'm going to pack a picnic lunch and walk up there. Why don't you come along?"

Alexander hesitated.

"Or are you ashamed to be seen with me?" Eliza asked. "A housemaid and a professor. People might stare."

"Oh, Eliza, you know it's not that. It's just—" Alexander broke off abruptly. "All right, I'll come."

"You pay a quarter for your lunch. I'll pay for mine. I don't want Miss Sadie to be out of pocket," Eliza said. Besides, she was feeling rich. Yesterday afternoon she had sent off the money she owed to Mrs. Endicott, and there was still some left over from this week's pay.

Alexander said little as they walked up over the

hills, but finally a deep compulsion to share his knowledge got the better of him. "See those tall trees with the straight brown trunks and the hanging cones? They're Douglas firs, and they sometimes grow to three hundred feet, higher than a tall building."

Eliza began to ask questions, and Alexander pointed out hemlocks with short, flat needles, sugar pine, ponderosa, and the aromatic cedars from which Seattle's house shingles were made. "I'm learning a bit about lumber at Yesler's," he said with a wry grin.

Walking ahead up a steep path, Eliza welcomed the thaw, ever so slight, in Alexander's frozen attitude of defeat. At the top of the hill she stopped and waited until he reached her side. "There's the lake, right below." Drawing in her breath in pure delight, she whispered, "Isn't it beautiful!"

Alexander's eyes swept the rippling water, lifted to the far shore, then came to rest on Eliza's face. "I've never known anyone with such a capacity for enjoyment," he said. "Don't you ever feel sorry for yourself?"

Eliza turned thoughtful. "Once I did," she admitted, "but that was a long time ago."

Half an hour later, seated on a fallen log at the lakeside, she brought up the idea suggested by Miss Sadie. "Imagine starting a school of your very own!"

"A secondary school, when I'm a qualified college teacher?"

"Yes, a secondary school." Eliza supposed, correctly, that he meant a high school. "What other choice have you? If you want to teach college students, you'll have to find means to train them yourself." Eliza found a more comfortable position on the log and leaned forward, resting her elbows on her knees. "In four years— only four years—you could be teaching your first college class."

Alexander could only look at the dark side. "In four years I'll be twenty-eight."

"Mr. Mercer's age," said Eliza. "That's not so old."

"I'd need other teachers. But more importantly, I'd need money. Eliza, you're daydreaming."

"I've thought of money," said Eliza. "First, you should go to Mr. Yesler. And if he turns you down, which he probably will, you should appeal to Doc Maynard to help you. He knows all the rich men in town."

Alexander turned and looked at Eliza in astonishment. "How do you know all this?"

"I *live* here," Eliza said.

For the first time in weeks, Alexander burst out laughing. "You're the limit. You really do intend to live here, don't you?"

"Of course. And so must you! You're *needed*. Have you ever thought of that? It's marvelous to be needed. I think it might be more satisfying than anything else in the world."

Alexander sat down, Indian fashion, on the pine needles at Eliza's feet. "I wonder if they'd let me have a couple of classrooms in the university?" he mused.

"Why not? Then they wouldn't go to waste."

"Who is this Doc Maynard?"

Eliza told him. "He could have made a fortune, Miss

Sadie says, but he gives most of his money away. He'll do anything to help Seattle grow and prosper. And I've thought of something else. Make a deal with Mr. Yesler. Tell him you'll work for him part-time, at a lower salary, if he'll help you get your school started. Oh, Alexander, I know you can do it! Please try."

Eliza talked on and on, becoming more eloquent by the moment. Finally Alexander held up his hands. "You've got me interested," he admitted. "Now keep quiet."

Getting up from the log, Eliza went down to the water's edge, where wild roses were blooming. She leaned down and sniffed their fragrance, then walked along the grassy bank until she reached a small clearing canopied in vines. Here she settled down on a patch of grass, rocking to and fro contentedly with her arms around her knees. He'll do it, she thought. He'll find some money, and some pupils, and the energy. All he needed was encouragement.

Not quite all. Alexander needed time alone to think things out, and Eliza gave it to him. For more than an hour she stayed in the little copse, watching fish jump in the water and listening to a thrush sing lustily from a tree above her head. Then she went back to where Alexander was still sitting on the bed of pine needles and matter-of-factly unpacked the lunch.

In the late afternoon the two walked back to Occidental Street, where the hotel was again alive with activity. Fewer girls were in evidence today, however, which made the presence of Thankful Turner and the black Irishman more noticeable.

Catching sight of Alexander, Thankful came down the steps from the porch. "Alex dear, do come here!" she called. "I want you to meet Mr. Cawtney Alsop!"

"Go ahead, Alex. I'll walk on." If Thankful was seriously involved with a new suitor, Eliza thought, Alexander might as well find out now. Then he could start afresh.

Yet Eliza asked him no questions about Thankful when he caught up with her. He was the one who said, "Thankful's got her heart's desire, a rich man to marry."

Eliza didn't pretend to be surprised, but she did wait anxiously for Alexander's reaction. Was he hurt? Was he jealous? Was he smoldering with righteous fury? How would a man feel if a beautiful girl like Thankful jilted him?

"I—I *am* sorry, Alex."

"Don't be," Alexander said. "It was all over from the moment Thankful got off the boat. I've had a couple of weeks to nurse my wounded pride, time enough to know I should count myself lucky."

"Lucky?" What a strange word for Alexander to use, thought Eliza.

"Yes, lucky. Thankful didn't come west to marry a schoolteacher. Eliza, you're a bright girl. You must have realized that."

"But you were together all the time."

Alexander chuckled. "She believed I'd saved her life, remember, and she wanted to give me a reward."

"I know that, but I thought she really liked you."

"I think she does, in a way. But the person she's really crazy about is—"

"Courtney Alsop?"

"No, herself."

"That's a harsh judgment," Eliza said, although she was inclined to agree.

"Not harsh, just tough-minded," contradicted Alexander. "It's a quality I'll need if I'm to succeed in this rough-and-tumble town, so I may as well start cultivating it."

To Eliza's relief, Alexander went to work with a purposeful stride the next morning, and after supper he talked for a long time with Miss Sadie about Doc Maynard and also about Arthur Denney, who had given Seattle the knoll on which the university building stood. He needed to know the names of every man who might be sufficiently interested in education to help financially. Then he began, during the long summer evenings, to approach each prospect in turn.

Sometimes he came back to the boardinghouse whistling, a cheerful sound Eliza came to recognize as she lay in bed. At other times he would report to Miss Sadie that one of his best prospects had turned out to be a stingy old coot who couldn't see the woods for the trees, but never once did he falter in his purpose.

On a very special evening when the moon hung over Mount Rainier like a giant gold coin he waited until Eliza had finished the dishes, then took her to see Yesler's Mill and the skid road down which teams of oxen dragged great logs from the mountains. "It's lumber money I'm after," he said. "Lumbering will not only build men's fortunes here, someday it will build a real university."

"A school where girls can go too?" asked Eliza.

"Why not?" asked Alexander, although he obviously thought the question astonishing. "If they're qualified." Then he changed the subject abruptly. "I forgot to tell you," he said, "that I sent a note by one of the schooner captains to a San Francisco bookstore. To see if they have a book on seashells, you know."

"For me?"

"Of course, for you."

Eliza wanted to hug him, but she was far too shy. Instead she stammered, "Wh-what a perfectly lovely thing to do!"

Alexander turned and looked down at her. "It's small thanks for what you've done for me." He took Eliza's hands, work-roughened from years of laundry and dishwashing, turned them so that the palms caught a glint of moonlight, then brought them up to his lips and kissed them tenderly. "You've given me a new lease on life, that's certain. And you may even have given me a career!"

Asa Mercer, after making a speech at Yesler Hall defending his tarnished reputation, took off for Oregon just before Thankful Turner was married to Courtney Alsop at the Occidental Hotel on the last day of June. It was a gala occasion. Evergreens and flowers banked a bridal arch, and all the important townspeople were invited. Thankful wore her grandmother's wedding veil of rosepoint lace, which she had thoughtfully brought along in her trunk, and Courtney wore a cut-away that smelled faintly of mothballs. There was a huge wedding breakfast (a dinner, actually) with roast suckling pig, cold salmon, and a haunch of beef. The Seattle Band played dance music, and untold numbers of Indians peered in every door and window, marveling at the sight of the white people's marriage ceremony.

Alexander reported back to Eliza and Miss Sadie that the bridegroom got drunk before the reception was half over and started singing barroom ballads. Thankful had behaved like a perfect lady through it all, but seemed decidedly relieved when the time came to climb in the Alsop carriage and start up the hill toward her new home.

"She'll have a time with that one," Miss Sadie predicted. "Nevertheless, I wish her joy."

"So do I," said Eliza with true sincerity. Then she added, thinking aloud, "She's so very far from home."

Later, after Miss Sadie said good-night and climbed the back stairs, Alexander asked, "Do you miss Salem, Eliza?"

"No." Eliza shuddered. "Do you still miss New York?"

"Sometimes," Alexander admitted, "but I think about the past less than I used to. I guess I'm getting the Seattle spirit. There's such a great future here, isn't there? For you and me."

Eliza Foster and Alexander Stenn were married on Midsummer Day a year later, after the school Alexander had started in the university building closed for summer vacation. Miss Sadie gave them a wedding reception in her big front room, and several of the Mercer girls came, along with all of the boarders. In later years Professor Stenn said that he owed his signal achievements in education to the encouragement of his wife. Mrs. Stenn, who by then had three children, was known to be one of the liveliest and most interesting women in Seattle. For her tenth anniversary she received a present from her husband that came by ship from San Francisco, a beautiful handmade cabinet to house the rare seashells she had been collecting over the years.

Author's Note

While Eliza and the characters with whom she is most closely associated are fictional, this story of the Mercer girls is based on the shipboard diary of Roger Conant, a *New York Times* reporter who accompanied Asa Mercer's expedition on a three-month voyage from New York through the Straits of Magellan to Seattle in 1866.* The background incidents and the timetable of the voyage on the S.S. *Continental*, a converted troop ship, are Mr. Conant's. A fifteen-year-old was the youngest girl on board, a sailor was lost overboard in the manner described, the incident with the Spanish man-of-war really happened, and at the Chilean port of Lota Mr. Mercer actually brandished a gun to protect his precious cargo. The fictional incidents that supplement the historical facts I have tried to make as close to the temper of the times as possible.

* *Mercer's Belles*, The Journal of a Reporter. Edited by Lenna A. Deutsch. Seattle: University of Washington Press, 1960.